'And what is worse,' said the Dream Master, 'you abandoned the dream right in the middle and let it go wandering off, goodness knows where, doing heaven knows what.' He slumped against the wall. 'We're in trouble,' he said. 'Twenty Types of Trouble – Double Mixed.'

Cy didn't say anything.

The little man was now chewing his beard and muttering. 'Of all the idiotic, irresponsible, irrational, ignorant ideas I've. . .' he paused for breath.

'Look,' Cy interrupted quickly. 'Is it really so bad?'

'Yes!' said the Dream Master. 'Do you know what they call a dream that's out of control?'

Cy shook his head.

'Let me be the one to tell you then,' said the dwarf. 'What we've got here is – a *Nightmare!*'

www.theresabreslin.co.uk

Also available in Corgi Yearling:

THE DREAM MASTER

This book is for HR, and he'll know why

When you dream,
where do you go?
Who decides where
the dream is to be - or
what is to happen? I am
a Dream Master and I
control the dreamworld,
follow the rules for a
good dream. For there
are rules - rules that
should not be
broken...

CHAPTER ·1·

'Move!' shrieked the girl as Cy skidded to a halt at the entrance to the house. She elbowed him hard in the back. 'Get inside! They're right behind us!'

There was a thud, and the sound of splintering wood as an axe crunched into the door just to the left of Cy's head.

'See?' the girl shouted right into Cy's face. 'Now come *on*!'

For the briefest second Cy hesitated. The girl pushed past him, flung the door open, then

grabbed his arm and dragged him inside.

'Put the bar across,' she ordered him, her bright blue eyes snapping with impatience, 'and then help me with Grandfather.'

Cy looked around helplessly. What bar? Across where?

The girl was by the hearth in the middle of the floor helping an old man to his feet. She glanced up at Cy. 'There!' she shrieked again, pointing to a wooden stave propped upright behind the door.

Cy lifted the piece of wood and clumsily slotted it into place. Just in time. There was a thunderous battering and the wooden planks of the door began to vibrate.

'We must hurry, Grandfather.' The girl spoke urgently but more gently. 'The raiders have come, and we must flee.'

The old man's voice was barely a whisper. 'Yes, but to where, daughter?'

Cy nodded in agreement. He was with the grandfather on this one. Exactly where were they going to escape to?

As if she had heard his thought, the girl looked at Cy. 'Go first,' she said, 'and open the way through to the pigpen.'

'Pigpen?' Cy stared at her stupidly. 'Where is the way to the pigpen?' he asked.

Cy hadn't thought it possible that she could screech even higher than she had before, but her voice moved up several decibels as she yelled at him.

'I don't believe it! A swineherd who does not know where the pigpen is? It is *that* way!' She had her grandfather's arm across her own shoulder and was trying to support him as they stumbled across the room.

'A swineherd!' cried Cy. 'Me a *swineherd*? No way!' He folded his arms across his chest. 'I am *not* being a swineherd.'

'What?' The girl stared at him.

Well, that had shut her up for a moment, thought Cy. Which gave him a bit of time to think things out. He hated having dreams like this, when everything seemed to be rolling along nicely – and then suddenly your dream took a nasty turn and there was nothing you could do about it. Well, he was not about to let that happen this time. He'd had previous experience in making his dreams go the way *he* wanted them to. It just took a bit of will-power and hard concentration. Cy shook his head in a determined manner. 'I am *not* being a swineherd,' he repeated.

'But you *are* a swineherd,' said the girl. 'You are Cy, the swineherd.'

'Oh yeah?' said Cy. 'And I suppose *you* are a princess?'

'Well . . . yes. I am Hilde, a Saxon princess of the royal house of Edgar.' The girl looked bewildered. 'But this you already know.'

'Ha!' said Cy. 'I thought so! You're a princess, and all I get to be is a swineherd. I *don't* think so.' He shook his head from side to side. He wasn't budging on this. Being a swineherd was certainly not in his dream plan. When he had first landed in this Viking dream Cy had decided at once that he should have a major part. He would march with the army of the English King Eadred to do battle against the Vikings at Stainmore, and try to drive them out of Northumbria. But then, just as the dream had started to get going, Cy had had a different idea. It had occurred to him that it might be a bit more exciting to be an actual Viking, or at least take part in a Viking raid. And no sooner had the thought clicked into place when suddenly he was running with this girl through wynds and alleyways in some medieval city.

Cy looked around him. Ending up in a cramped hovel, accompanied by an old man and a bossy girl, being pursued by bloodthirsty barbarians was certainly not what he had intended. This dream was going way off course.

'You are what you are,' said Hilde. 'A swineherd.'

'Nope,' said Cy. 'Not this time. This is *my* dream, so I am what I want to be.'

'Your *dream*,' Hilde repeated in disbelief. 'You think this is a *dream*?'

'It's not an *ordinary* dream,' explained Cy. 'Usually when you dream, your dreams are inside your head. But with this,' he held up his piece of dreamsilk, 'it works the other way about. It's part of my Dream Master's dreamcloak. Using it, I can take myself right *inside my own dream*. So now I'm practising being a Dream Master. This is *my* dream, which means *I* decide what happens . . .'

Cy's voice faltered for a second. He had just remembered that his Dream Master had warned him that he should NEVER switch characters or storylines in the middle of a dream.

'Stories are very powerful things,' the little man had once told him. 'Don't mess with them, or it can end up an absolute disaster. Look what happened with the *Titanic*.'

'But that actually *did* really happen,' Cy had protested.

The Dream Master had shuddered. 'Exactly,' he said.

Thank goodness the little dwarf wasn't here to criticize him, thought Cy. Helped by his own tiny piece of torn dreamsilk Cy was managing just fine on his own. Who needed the crabby dwarf with his dreamcloak? Now ... if he could get a minute's peace from this girl ... Already she was opening her mouth to speak again. Cy held up his hand. 'Shush,' he said, 'until I think up what happens next.'

'Others have already decided what is happening here,' cried Hilde. She stepped forward and viciously kicked open the lattice gate which led to the backyard. 'Now come and help me with my grandfather.'

'Hang on a minute,' said Cy. He was about to point out that dumb the Vikings weren't, and by now it would probably have occurred to their pursuers to run round to the back of the house, when he stopped and sniffed the air. There was an odd, dangerous smell stinging his nostrils, and then a crackling noise came from above his head. Cy looked up.

'Omigosh!' he yelped.

The raiders had thought of a simpler way of

forcing them out of the house. The roof was on fire.

'The roof's on fire!' Cy shouted.

'Well, there's a surprise,' said Hilde sarcastically. 'Who would have thought it? The Vikings have only done that to every single other settlement all along this coast.' She turned round and glared at Cy. 'Fear has addled your wits, swineherd,' she said, 'and I cannot care for both you and grandfather. So, follow on while I try to get him by the path to the river, or . . .' she glanced up at the roof and then at Cy, '. . . stay here and burn.' She bent down and squirmed through the low opening in the back wall.

Cy stopped in the centre of the room. 'No,' he told himself resolutely. 'I *am* going to change this dream. It just needs some proper concentration.' He screwed up his face and thought as hard as he could. This was what he was good at. Everybody said so: his teacher, friends, family. There wasn't much else he could do without falling over his feet. But making up stories was his best subject. His Grampa always told him that he had a great imagination. So, he would use it now and dream up a better scene than this. After a few seconds Cy opened his eyes.

Thick smoke was pouring down into the room,

and red flames were reaching out along the roof beams. Cy was about to close his eyes and try again when, with a great shattering crash, the door to the street split apart.

A tall bearded Viking warrior stood in the doorway brandishing a shield and a sword. On his head he wore a helmet, a heavy metal helmet with earflaps and a long flat central nose-piece. From within the eye sockets two eyes stared out with murderous intent.

The Viking raised his sword, roared his war-cry and sprang forwards. At that moment part of the roof beam fell down felling him to the ground and sending a shower of burning sparks over Cy.

Cy screamed and ran for the lattice gate. As he dived through he felt the most almighty horrid crack as his head connected with the door lintel.

'Owww!' he cried.

CHAPTER·2·

'Owww!!!'

Mrs Chalmers, Cy's class teacher, shot up out of her seat at the front of the bus. She turned around and held up the paper ball which had just bounced off the top of her head. 'Who threw this?' she demanded.

All down the bus her pupils were sprawled out across the seats, reading comics, chewing sweets, and shouting insults at each other.

'Uh?' said the two nearest to her.

Mrs Chalmers grabbed the P.A. microphone.

'Quieten down, everyone!' she shouted above the din. 'Now,' she continued, when there was a silence, 'I warned all of you before we left to go to York. If we are going to survive a week-long trip together then there must be no unruly behaviour. So . . .' she held up the scrunched-up sandwich bag, 'did anyone see who threw this piece of paper?'

Cy's classmates looked at each other. Even if they *had* seen anything, nobody was going to tell.

'It's really not good enough.' Mrs Chalmers began to walk up the aisle of the bus. 'If this missile had hit the driver, then he could easily have been distracted. You are old enough to know that's very dangerous.' She looked around her. 'The guilty person should own up.'

Cy glanced across the aisle at Eddie and Chloe. His eyes had snapped open a few seconds earlier, and he knew exactly which one of them had lobbed the scrunched-up piece of paper to the front of the bus. He also knew that there was no way that these two class bullies, known to everyone as the Mean Machines, were going to admit to it.

'Is nobody going to say who did this?' Mrs Chalmers had reached Cy's seat.

Cy's eyes caught Chloe's gaze. She stared across at him and narrowed her eyes, daring him to tell on her. Then suddenly Chloe gave Cy a bright wicked smile. She leaned into the passageway.

'Mrs Chalmers,' she said in a voice so low that only Cy and Mrs Chalmers could hear.

Mrs Chalmers bent down a little.

'I think . . .' Chloe hesitated.

'Yes, Chloe?' Mrs Chalmers prompted quietly.

Chloe chewed her lip uncomfortably for a second or two and then spoke in a sincere worried voice. 'I think that Cy might have something to tell you, but . . .' she pulled at Mrs Chalmers' coat-sleeve, '. . . perhaps later, when there's nobody else about.'

Mrs Chalmers straightened up. 'Thank you, Chloe,' she said. 'It's very brave of you to speak up.' She turned and looked down at Cy. 'Cy, I won't tolerate rough horseplay on the bus.' Her mouth set in a severe line. 'I'll speak to you when we arrive at the hostel in York.'

Cy gasped. It had happened again! He knew that the Mean Machines were very smart at not getting caught picking on people. But this time they had gone even further! Without actually saying so, Chloe had made it seem that *he* had

17

chucked the paper ball down to the front of the bus. And now, if he told on them, then he would be a sneak and a grass. What was he going to say to Mrs Chalmers when they arrived at the hostel in York?

His teacher walked briskly back to her own seat. Cy, his face red, stared out of the bus window, past Innes who had fallen asleep beside him. He had really wanted to go on this school trip, but he was already in trouble before it had even properly begun!

'The Viking, Erik Bloodaxe, who ruled York many years ago, was so called for obvious reasons . . .' Cy's teacher had picked up the P.A. microphone again, and was reading from one of the history books she had brought with her.

Cy kept his back firmly turned away from Chloe and Eddie sitting opposite. 'Ignore bullies as much as you can,' his Grampa had advised him. 'They get a buzz from annoying people, so you've got to try and spoil their game by not getting annoyed.' Cy tried to keep his mind on what Mrs Chalmers was saying.

'In the Middle Ages people lived in constant fear of the Nordic raiders from the sea,' Mrs Chalmers went on. 'The Vikings were very skilled in building ships and were great sailors. They came sweeping down the coast of Britain looking for plunder, setting fire to the towns and villages.'

Yeah, right, Cy smiled to himself. Don't I know it. He pulled his piece of dreamsilk from where he'd had it tucked up his sleeve. It had been the last thing he'd grabbed from home before he'd set out on the school trip this Monday morning. He didn't think he could safely leave it, even hidden under his chest of drawers. Not if he was going to be away for a whole week, and especially not if his dad was talking about *maybe* redecorating Cy's bedroom while he was gone. Cy looked at it carefully. Because it had been in contact with his skin, it must have triggered the illusion that his dream was real. It was pale and grey, and looked worn out.

It couldn't have worked like that, could it? Not such a tiny piece, to make his Viking dream so real. It needed Cy's own Dream Master with his dreamcloak. Didn't it?

Anyway, Cy thought, if he ever did get back there, then he would have to sort that particular story out. He couldn't have some narky girl butting in, ordering him about, and doing the rescuing bit.

He stuffed the torn cloth into his trouser pocket. Then he reached out to the seat pocket in front of him to get his comic to read. His hand stopped in mid-air, and his eyes opened wide. His fingers were smeared with soot. Cy held up his other hand. It too was streaked with black marks. Then Cy noticed the sleeve of his sweatshirt. Slowly he brought it closer to his face. There were tiny holes on the sleeve, on both sleeves, and . . . and . . . Cy bent his chin and looked down. All down his front were spattered little irregular burn marks . . . as if a shower of sparks from a fire had landed on him.

CHAPTER·3·

It wasn't until later that evening when everybody was settled in the school hostel accommodation that Cy got a chance to take a really good look at his sweatshirt. He examined the surface closely, and then stuck his little finger through one of the larger holes. They were definitely burn marks, but how could that be? Cy looked again at the piece of dreamsilk. It seemed different somehow, deeper, darker ... almost liquid in the way it flowed through his fingers. He would have to make absolutely sure that he had no

direct contact with it when he fell asleep. If even such a small piece of dreamsilk was so powerful, then he would have to keep it right out the way. Cy touched it cautiously. He wasn't going near it again. Then he grinned to himself. Well, at least until he had a clearer idea of the direction that he wanted his Viking dream to take.

'You've to report to Mrs Chalmers.' Basra appeared beside Cy's bed. 'She's in the office downstairs.' He gave Cy a sympathetic look. 'I'll walk down with you,' he offered.

Cy looked up. Eddie was lounging in the dormitory doorway. Cy stuffed the sweatshirt and the dreamsilk to the bottom of his holdall, and then shoved the bag under his bed. 'Yeah, great. Thanks, Basra.'

'Don't go green,' Eddie hissed as Cy passed him.

'What's he on about?' asked Basra.

'He's warning me not to grass them up,' said Cy. 'It was the Mean Machines who bounced the paper ball off Mrs Chalmers's head on the bus.'

Basra groaned. 'Might have known,' he said. 'They don't know what to be up to, do they? I hope they're not going to ruin this trip for the rest of us.' He punched Cy on the shoulder. They had reached the office. 'Good luck,' he said.

Mrs Chalmers was sitting behind the hostel manager's desk. 'Cy,' she said severely, 'chucking stuff around on a moving bus is not on. We're going to be using the bus a lot during this week. I have to be sure it won't happen again.'

Cy could feel the old familiar panic which always started inside him when he was stressed: the shaky fluttering which centred in his head and stopped him thinking straight. He took a big breath and tried one of Grampa's 'Panic Prevention Practices' – counting backwards very slowly from eleven.

'I didn't do it, miss,' he managed to say eventually.

'There has been an indication that you did.'

Cy shook his head miserably.

Mrs Chalmers sighed. 'You wouldn't then like to tell me who actually did do it?'

Cy shook his head again. His brain had blipped out of action. Now he couldn't speak at all, even if he wanted to. He hated it when this happened. His clumsiness seemed to seep right through him and take over his whole body.

Mrs Chalmers looked up at the ceiling and then she looked back at Cy. She knew that he often got himself into difficult situations, but he always owned up when he'd done something wrong. Whereas Chloe, now that she thought about it, could be a mischief-maker. What to do? she asked herself. What to do?

Cy stared at his teacher. It was awful being so awkward, so cack-handed, so gauche . . . Suddenly Cy had a blinding flash of inspiration. 'Mrs Chalmers,' he said seriously, 'you *know* that it couldn't possibly have been me who threw the paper ball at you.'

Mrs Chalmers raised her eyebrows.

Cy gave her a weak smile. 'If I had thrown it,' he said, 'it would have missed.'

There was a silence. Then Mrs Chalmers laughed out loud. 'Yes, Cy,' she said. 'I take your point. Your co-ordination is not always one hundred per cent.' She stood up. 'Enough of this,' she said briskly. 'Whatever else you do or do not excel at, Cyrus Peters, you have never been a liar. If you say that you did not do it, then I believe you. Tonight, at dinner, I will tell everyone that it must never happen again. And we will forget all about the incident. This time . . .' she called after Cy as he went out the door. 'Which makes me realize,' she added quietly to herself when Cy had left, 'exactly what Miss Chloe was playing at when she spoke to me.'

*

After dinner was cleared away, Mrs Chalmers and the other teachers gave out the programme for the week. There were to be excursions every day to places like the Railway Museum, the Jorvik Centre, the Minster and the Castle Museum. Tomorrow they would have an introductory historical tour and walk the City walls.

'And then, because you will all have absorbed so much culture and knowledge during the day, you will be able to write about it in the evening.'

At once, everybody began to moan.

'That sounds like schoolwork to me,' said Vicky, who was sitting on the window-ledge beside Cy and the rest of their friends.

'Too right,' said Cy.

'It will be fun,' said Mrs Chalmers.

There were some whistles and catcalls. Cy noticed that the other teachers, Mr Gillespie and Ms Tyler, were joining in.

Mrs Chalmers held up her hand for silence. 'No, really, I mean it. I have arranged for a local theatre group to come along and do workshops with us. We will provide the story and Matt, their director, will help us produce a play together. It will be performed on Thursday evening, the last night before we leave. Pupils from the local primary school have been invited to come along and watch.'

'Are we charging them for tickets?' asked Basra.

'More likely they'll charge *us*,' said Cy.

'Can we have auditions?' Vicky called out.

'Tomorrow,' said Mrs Chalmers. 'The auditions will be tomorrow. First, we need a starting point.' She looked around the hall. 'Any suggestions as to what we might write about?'

'Duh,' said Vicky. She crossed her eyes at Cy. 'Duh . . .' she said again. 'As we *are* in York, I suggest . . . a play about the . . . er . . . Vikings?'

'Oh, well done, Vicky!' said Mrs Chalmers. 'That's exactly what I was going to say, and it just so happens that we've brought lots of materials on the Vikings with us. Excellent, that's settled then,' she said cheerfully. 'You can all have twenty minutes to write and then get off to bed as we've been travelling most of the day. Tomorrow I want some interesting ideas for a story.'

Cy tried to have another good think before he switched off the lamp by his bed. His notebook was beside him, and already it was covered in scribbles. He liked to write his story ideas down quickly, just as they came into his head. If he tried to make up proper sentences he found that the ideas stopped coming. And anyway, he wasn't good at long bursts of actual writing. When he had to write things down in class, his words always struggled to stay on the line ... and failed. They usually gave up eventually and fell right off. It showed up how bad his co-ordination was. Adults usually tutted or heaved a sigh when they looked at his exercise book.

Cy found that his mind kept going back to the Viking dream which he'd had on the bus. Well, he decided, if he was going to write *that* story there were a few things that would need changing. For a start off, if anyone was going to do any rescuing or brave deeds, it was going to be him, Cy, and not some cranky girl who said she was a princess. She – what was her name again? – Hilde, yes, well *she* could be a swineherd, or herdess, or Little Bo Peep even. Cy fell asleep smiling, thinking of Hilde trying to round up several dozen crazy sheep, two of whom looked very like Eddie and Chloe.

CHAPTER·4·

'The walls surrounding the city of York are the best place to start any exploration of the city.'

It was the following morning and Cy was with the rest of the class at the foot of some steps at the start of their historic walk around the city.

'We will begin here,' continued their guide, 'and I'll stop from time to time to point out anything interesting as we walk the walls.'

An early morning mist still hung in the air and the creamy stone of the Minster glowed in the faint

sunlight. As they went along the guide talked about how the Romans had established the city of Eburacum between the rivers Ouse and Foss.

'Over the years it became a busy place for trading: furs, walrus, ivory and other goods. It had many buildings of wattle and timber, and was known to the Vikings as Jorvik.'

Cy could just make out the broad river, with people strolling on the pathways alongside.

'It's hard to imagine,' said the guide, 'that this area would have been very busy with traders and of course the famous Viking longships.'

No, thought Cy, it isn't hard to imagine them at all. He squinted out across the water, screwing up his eyes against the thousand shimmering droplets in the air and their reflections on the waves. The mist rising made it difficult to make out anything other than dull shapes in the distance.

'We will move on,' said the guide, and Cy's class began to follow her along the parapet.

Suddenly the sun broke through the haze and Cy stopped with a gasp. The dazzling light gleamed on the river and off the prows of a dozen or so longships. Their dragon figureheads arched proudly as they slid through the water. Cy gripped the edge of the stone wall.

'Come on, Cy,' called Mrs Chalmers. 'Keep up please.'

Cy turned. His school party was crocodiling along further ahead of him. Their guide was at the end of the line waiting for him.

'What's wrong?' she asked, as Cy rushed up.

'In the river!' cried Cy. He pointed across the ramparts. 'I saw Viking longships in the river!'

'Oh yes,' said the guide. 'They put on pageants at different times of the year. They're probably practising today.' She leaned out to have a look. Then she turned and grinned at Cy. 'Nice,' she said. 'You really got me with that one.'

Cy went to the wall and looked out again. There was nothing on the river except a tourist barge. He could hear the tannoyed voice of its guide faintly in the distance. Cy's heart jumped. What had he seen? Or what had he thought he'd seen?

'Come *along*, Cy,' Mrs Chalmers called impatiently.

Cy glanced back and then hurried to catch up. His head was still swimmy when they reached the Castle Museum.

'It's so oppressive today,' said the guide as she led them inside. 'We need some heavy rain to clear the atmosphere.'

It wasn't much better inside the museum. The air seemed treacly and the light hazy. To Cy everything seemed indistinct, as though the objects hadn't been drawn in clearly enough. Hardly listening he followed the person in front of him on the tour.

'This is the Viking helmet discovered a few years ago in one of the main streets of York, known as the foregate.' Their guide had paused in front of an exhibit. 'It is made of iron and brass, and if you look carefully you can see a name inscribed on it. No-one knows how or why it was buried there. You can see a hologram of it at the Jorvik Centre.'

Cy moved closer. There was the inscription . . . some strange lettering . . . He leaned in to get a better look. His eyes watered and his head spun. There was something odd happening . . . drifting mist in front of his eyes . . . and in it he could see . . . the domed crown, the nose-guard, the intricate design . . .

And then Cy felt the air closing in around him. A dizzy feeling and . . . a sudden sense of danger. His throat tightened and his brain faltered. What? Under the visor a head was taking shape. The face was lined and hard, chin set with purpose. It was that of a Viking warrior. And from within the eye sockets the eyes, mad with rage, stared out at him.

'Cy!' Mrs Chalmers called sharply. 'Are you all right?'

'Yes. No. I think so.' Cy put his hand across his eyes. 'I don't know.'

Mrs Chalmers took his arm and led him to a chair. 'Sit down, and I'll fetch a glass of water. It's probably just the heat,' she said. She wafted her hand in front of her face. 'It *is* very hot in here.'

The lights in the museum flickered.

'Electrical storm,' said the guide. 'The air is so heavy today. When the weather builds up like this it can cause power surges. Nothing to worry about.'

The very next second the museum fire alarm went off.

'Blast!' said the guide. 'It's probably a short circuit, but we must go out. Now!' She began to usher the class towards the door.

Cy got up as Mrs Chalmers hurried back to the group.

'Good,' she said. 'You all know how to follow a fire drill. Be sensible. Nearest fire exit as fast as you can, and we will assemble outside.'

The air seemed thicker and heavier with each

step Cy took. He pushed open a door marked 'Fire Exit', stumbled down some stairs and out into . . . thick smoke pouring from the burning thatch of the house across the way.

So it hadn't been a false alarm, Cy thought. The museum really was on fire. He staggered down the street and turned to look back at the building. His mouth dropped open. The museum wasn't there. In its place were stables. Cy looked around wildly. Everywhere was flame and fire. He could hear the noise of the terrified animals trapped in the burning building. Then he heard running feet, and people screaming.

Cy saw an alleyway and scurried into it. Halfway down he stopped to catch his breath. He didn't know how it had happened, but he knew without doubt that he was back in his Viking dream!

Cy looked around him desperately. What should he do? Where could he go?

Suddenly he heard a familiar voice.

'Thundering Thor!' it shouted. 'What in the Name of Nineteen Norsemen do you think you are doing?'

CHAPTER·5·

'**D**ream Master!' cried Cy.

A little man with a wizened face and a beard was standing in the alleyway. He had his arms folded across his chest and a furious expression on his face.

'Explain this!' he demanded.

'Er . . . what?' said Cy.

'*I* am your Dream Master. You cannot have a dream without me being there. Dreams need Dream Masters. How is it that you are in a dream that I know nothing about? You cannot move in

and out of the Dreamworld without my help.'

'You mean this Viking dream? It was all a mistake,' babbled Cy. 'The last time we met, when I grabbed your dreamcloak, a piece tore off and I still have it. I didn't mean to use it – honestly. I was going off on the school trip to York, and I tucked the bit of your dreamcloak up my sleeve. It was to keep it safe, in case my mum or dad found it when I was away. Then I fell asleep on the bus, and the next thing I knew I was being chased by Vikings, and then I ran into a house and they set it on fire.'

'And?' prompted the Dream Master.

'Then I woke up, and when I realized that I had sort of Dream Mastered my own dream by mistake, I put the piece of dreamsilk away. At once,' Cy added.

A couple of terrified pigs came squealing and grunting down the alley. The Dream Master grabbed Cy and hauled him out of the way.

'So how did you get back into Viking times just now?'

'I don't know,' said Cy. 'We were being shown round the museum. Everything was strange, the light was blurred and the air was syrupy. I couldn't breathe. The fire alarm went off. I don't know why . . .'

'In case you haven't noticed,' the Dream Master pointed to the roofs of the houses opposite, 'the whole town is burning.'

'Yes,' said Cy. '*Here* it is, because the Vikings set it on fire. But it wasn't, not where I was originally. They said that the fire alarm had gone off due to an electrical fault.'

'So how exactly did you arrive into this TimeSpace?' asked the Dream Master.

'I don't know,' said Cy. 'It just happened.'

The Dream Master frowned. 'Dreams don't just *happen*,' he said testily. 'And not like this either.' He waved his hand about. 'This one is drifting about all over York. I was fishing quietly down by the river when suddenly half a dozen Viking long-ships appeared out of nowhere.'

'I saw them too!' cried Cy. 'So I didn't imagine them!'

The Dream Master gave Cy a strange look. 'You probably *did*, actually.' He waved his hand in the air, as Cy opened his mouth. 'We'll go into that later,' he said hurriedly. Then he looked at Cy and spoke seriously. 'This dream is wafting about any old where, through Time and Space. And what's worrying is that it looks as though it's beginning to seep through to the twenty-first century.' He shook his head. 'We can't have this. Dreams should be contained inside the dreamer's head. This one appears to be *leaking*. It's very dangerous. Also,' the Dream Master squinted through the haze, 'there's something not quite *right* about all of it.'

Cy looked around him. He knew what the Dream Master meant. The sounds of the fire and the flames burning were odd and unreal.

The Dream Master turned abruptly to Cy. 'Who is dreamweaving?'

'Eh?' said Cy.

'Where is this dream's Dream Master?' said the dwarf. 'It can't be you. You don't have the piece of my cloak in your hand. It's not me. My own dreamcloak is still.' He moved his wrist like a matador with a cape. 'Look.'

Cy could see that the Dream Master's dream-cloak was almost translucent.

'There are no dreams moving in there just now.' The dwarf frowned. 'It's as if ... as if ...' The Dream Master stared at Cy, and Cy saw fear on his face. 'It's as if *no-one* is in control. As if this dream is going along by itself. How can that be?'

Cy dropped his eyes.

The Dream Master stepped forward and thrust his face close to Cy's own. 'I want you to tell me *exactly* what happened when you fell asleep, dreaming, on the bus, with a piece of my dreamcloak.'

Cy gulped. 'I knew as soon as I was in the dream, that it wasn't an ordinary dream. The dream wasn't inside my head as dreams normally are. It was *me* that was actually *inside* the dream. And we were going to York, and Mrs Chalmers had been telling us about the Vikings, so . . .'

The dwarf nodded impatiently. 'Yes, yes, yes.'

'Well,' said Cy, 'I thought a Viking adventure would be great, and . . . and . . . I'd have a shot at being a Dream Master.'

The dwarf struck his own forehead with his fist. 'You don't "have a shot at" being a Dream Master. It takes Ages of training and experience. And when I say "Ages" that's exactly what I mean. Like "the Stone Age" or "the Middle Ages". Well, go on.' He glared at Cy.

'To begin with,' said Cy, 'I decided to dream that I would go with the army of King Eadred who were marching to Stainmore to fight Erik Bloodaxe. But that got a bit boring. Do you know that the soldiers only eat twice a day and it is the same food each time? And when you need to go to the toilet you just do it, like . . . *anywhere*?'

'Get to the point!'

'Well, anyway,' said Cy, 'it was pretty boring. So I thought it would be more exciting to be with the Vikings for a bit, so I decided I would just change the story—'

'CHANGE THE STORY!' bawled the Dream Master. 'Don't tell me you tried to make the story go in a way that it shouldn't?'

'We-ell . . . I suppose so,' stammered Cy.

'Are you out of your mind?'

'I thought it might work,' said Cy.

The Dream Master flung his hands in the air. 'Of course it's *not* going to work. Not properly anyway. You can't change a story's pattern.'

'Isn't it like editing?' suggested Cy.

'No, it is NOT like editing,' said the Dream Master fiercely. 'Editing is when you take out the bits that should never have been there in the first place, and put in the parts that should have.'

'Doesn't a Dream Master make up the story as the dream goes along?' asked Cy. 'And if you don't,' he went on doggedly, 'then you're not actually Master of the Dream, are you? You're more of an observer.'

'How dare you!' spluttered the dwarf. 'Of course I am Master of the Dream. A story needs a narrator or a writer. Everybody makes up stories, even people who think they can't. You do it. In fact . . .' he dodged to one side as a burning brand fell off the roof above, narrowly missed him and fell hissing into a barrel of water, 'you have a very vivid imagination. But a story is a course of events which *lead somewhere*. It should have a beginning, a middle, and an end – usually, but not always, in that order. And you do NOT go around messing with a story's fundamentals. They don't like it. A good story goes its own way. Do they teach you NOTHING at school? I thought they had some kind of literacy hour in the twenty-first century. What's that all about?'

Cy shrugged his shoulders. 'Search me.'

'And what is worse,' said the Dream Master, 'you abandoned it right in the middle and let it go wandering off, goodness knows where, doing heaven knows what.' He slumped against the wall. 'We're in trouble,' he said. 'Twenty Types of Trouble – Double Mixed.'

Cy didn't say anything.

The little man was now chewing his beard and muttering. 'Of all the idiotic, irresponsible, irrational, ignorant ideas I've . . .' he paused for breath.

'Look,' Cy interrupted quickly. 'Is it really so bad?'

'Yes!' said the Dream Master. 'Do you know what they call a dream that's out of control?'

Cy shook his head.

'Let me be the one to tell you then,' said the dwarf. 'What we've got here is – a *Nightmare!*'

CHAPTER·6·

'I ve had nightmares before,' Cy said bravely. 'Oh yes?' replied the Dream Master. 'And can you recall how they ended? Huh?'

Cy thought for a moment. 'Well . . . usually with something pretty awful,' he admitted. From somewhere nearby they heard the clash of metal and the noise of fighting. 'But that's not going to happen here,' Cy glanced anxiously at the Dream Master, 'is it?'

'I don't know,' said the Dream Master. 'After all, this dream was started off by *you*, without

any consultation whatsoever with *me*.'

'Couldn't we just leave it to sort itself out?' asked Cy.

'Don't be so irresponsible,' said the Dream Master. 'You can't have unfinished stories just wandering off. Goodness knows what would happen to them. This one is floating about all over the place, and it's causing trouble already. See?' He held up his dreamcloak, and through its folds Cy could dimly see York in the twenty-first century. Buses, vans, cars, and bicycles jostled on the streets. Little clusters of tourists dutifully followed their guides about.

'What?' asked Cy.

'Look more closely,' snapped the Dream Master.

Cy looked again into the rippling depths of the dreamsilk. The city tour bus had paused nearby, and just in front of it was a very large man waving his arms over his head. Cy peered closer. The figure stumbling about in the traffic was dressed in a mail tunic with rough trousers bound with cross-garters. He had dropped his axe and clapped his hands over his ears, his eyes popping with fear and panic. Horns were beeping and motorists shouting. An old lady darted out into the middle of the road. She grabbed the man's arm and guided him to the safety of the pavement opposite. Then she turned and shook her fist at the nearest car. 'Road rage!' she shouted.

'Omigosh!' said Cy. 'He's not an actor dressed up for a part, is he?'

The dwarf shook his head. 'He is as real as the Viking ships you saw in the estuary this morning. Your Viking dream is adrift, and you'll need to do something – fast!'

'This story won't just sort itself out then.' Cy's remark was a statement rather than a question. Through the dreamcloak he could still see the Viking who was now surrounded by a bunch of tourists furiously clicking their cameras. 'Things *are* getting a little bit mixed up,' he admitted.

'A *little* bit mixed up!' exploded the dwarf. 'That is the most understated of understatements ever uttered. I suppose you would have called World War Two a "bit of an argument". Listen, you . . . you . . . nincompoop, you'd better get it into your noodle-headed noddle just how bad this is. Forget "Mixed Up". Substitute "Shambles". Try "Havoc". Think "Chaos". There is *no* end to what could happen to this. Stories are fuelled on the most powerful energy in the universe . . . *imagination*.'

Suddenly Cy remembered a conversation he'd

had with his Grampa about the future. 'The most exciting discoveries are still to come,' Cy's Grampa had said, and then he'd leaned over and tapped Cy gently on the head. 'It's all inside there, contained in the human brain. Remember Einstein's quote: "Imagination is everything".'

'Einstein said "Imagination is everything",' said Cy.

'Yes,' said the Dream Master. 'And being Einstein he meant *precisely* what he said ... Imagination *is* E-V-E-R-Y-T-H-I-N-G.' The little dwarf pronounced each syllable separately.

'You mean ... there is no limit on it?' Cy asked slowly.

'None. Your imagination can produce what is, what is not, and ...' the expression on the dwarf's face again became fearful ... 'and *what can never be.*'

Cy frowned hard as his brain tried to take this in.

'We have to find a way to solve this problem,' said the dwarf in a worried voice, 'otherwise this Story could end up anywhere. And I do mean *any*where. Supposing it bangs into somebody's unfinished novel about a series of intergalactic wars? Or it encounters an incomplete haiku poem?' The dwarf had worked himself into a rage and was now biting his beard furiously. 'Bumbleheaded Boy!' he shouted.

'Yelling at me won't help,' said Cy. 'It makes me feel worse, actually.'

'Pardon *me*,' said the dwarf, 'if I am making *you* feel worse. But, if I'm not mistaken, it *was* you who triggered this off. Remember? So—'

'—it will have to be me who fixes it,' Cy finished for him. 'OK. Any ideas as to how I do it?'

The dwarf twisted round and stared into his dreamcloak for a moment. He turned back, and avoided looking directly at Cy. 'The matter requires some thought,' he said carefully.

'You mean, you don't know what to do?' asked Cy.

'I am developing a strategy,' said the dwarf.

'Omigosh,' said Cy. 'You *really* don't know what to do.'

'Of course I know what to do,' said the dwarf testily. 'I'm thinking it through first. You mustn't rush off and do something silly. But what I have to do *first* is to nip through TimeSpace, retrieve that Viking warrior, and return him to the part of the dream that he fell through, before someone in twenty-first-century York calls the emergency services. Although,' he gave Cy a severe look, 'it appears to be the custom in your century to allow confused people who need help to live on the streets.' He swung his dreamcloak and disappeared.

That was a bit unfair, thought Cy. It's the adults who always make the decisions here. And things hadn't got any better with almost everybody having self-government either. Perhaps what was really needed was a *children's* Parliament. He leaned against the wall. His legs were wobbly, and his head ached. Perhaps he'd breathed in too much smoke, but ... he drew his hand across his eyes, the smoke seemed to have cleared. The air was fresher. The sun was shining, the mist from this morning had almost cleared. Through the dreamwisps Cy could see Ms Tyler, Mr Gillespie, and Mrs Chalmers walking up and down the street ticking off names. Any minute now they were going to miss him. The way he felt at the moment Cy didn't much care.

Mr Gillespie walked right past him and then glanced back. 'Oh, Cy, there you are. I didn't see you for a moment.' He ticked Cy's name on his list, and then took him firmly by the arm. 'Right, that's us all accounted for,' he told Mrs Chalmers.

'Come along, everybody,' called Mrs Chalmers. 'I want to organize lunch now.'

Cy looked behind him down the long narrow street. He could see his dream rolling away from him. Where was his Dream Master?

'Come *on*, Cy,' called Mrs Chalmers, 'stop dreaming.'

'I wish I could,' Cy muttered under his breath as he hurried to catch up.

CHAPTER ·7·

Ms Tyler and Mr Gillespie had organized a game of rounders on the school hostel playing-fields after dinner that evening. Cy had never been very good at games of this kind, and was glad that he had the excuse of not feeling well earlier, which meant that he could sit and watch the others.

His brain was twanging inside his skull as he tried to work out what to do for the best. He knew that someone had to make sure that the Viking story was ended properly. And that someone was

most definitely him. But the Dream Master had told Cy to do nothing until *he* had decided what was to happen. So he should wait until the little man turned up again. But now Cy was getting edgy, and he didn't really know why. The air was strange again, it had a sheen which hurt his eyes and stopped him looking directly at anyone or anything.

'What do you mean you can't find it?' Mr Gillespie called out to Innes. 'That's the third ball that's gone astray among those same bushes. Is there a black hole down there that they are all disappearing into?'

Cy glanced over to where the commotion was. The sun was casting long shadows and he could see Innes and Basra kicking about in the undergrowth, trying to find the lost ball. There was a fine thin mist rising from the river, and twisting slowly through the trees across the fields. Fog from the North Sea, a haar that muffled the noise of the oars and hid the longships so that you did not see them until it was too late: the boats with the carved prows which streaked through the water, shallow-bottomed so that they could beach quickly, high up on the shore line. Then the warriors would leap down with great shouts and terrifying yells . . .

Cy stood up quickly. Shadows without substance were moving down by the riverbank. One in particular was taller than the rest, a huge warrior; cloaked . . . helmeted . . . As Cy stared, the figure raised his axe high above his head. Faintly, yet distinctly, Cy heard his battle-cry.

'I think we should go in now!' Cy's voice came out breathless and ragged.

'Did Mrs Chalmers call?' Ms Tyler turned and asked Cy.

Cy crossed his fingers behind his back. 'I thought I heard someone shout.' That part was true, at least.

Ms Tyler looked at her watch. 'You're probably right, Cy. Perhaps the theatre group have arrived early.' She waved to the others. 'Time to pack up and go in.'

Fortunately the theatre group had arrived, and had already begun to arrange equipment and props on the stage at the far end of the dining hall. Mrs Chalmers was drawing out a storyboard on a blackboard.

'Everybody get their notepads please,' she called, 'and sharpen your pencils and your brains before you sit down.'

Cy raced upstairs to get his notebook, and saw

his holdall jutting out from under his bed. He opened it, grabbed his notepad and pencil and then kicked it firmly right back underneath the bed. He certainly was not going to touch the piece of dreamsilk at the moment. Not until the Dream Master reappeared and told him what to do. As he ran back downstairs Cy almost bumped into Eddie and Chloe giggling together outside the dining-hall door. He walked quickly past them. The Mean Machines were definitely up to something. All that whispering and nudging usually meant that a victim was being picked out for some future nasti-ness or teasing that always went too far.

Matt, the director of the theatre group, had organized a running order to hear everyone read out their story ideas. Cy watched and listened, and grew more nervous as the queue shortened and it got nearer to his turn. He desperately wanted a part in the play, but he knew that he was so useless when it came to reading aloud. It didn't help either that, for some reason, Eddie and Chloe had decided to sit right alongside him. This meant that they would be called after him, and so gave them a good chance to snigger when Cy was speaking. Already they were tittering behind their hands. Cy felt himself grow hot.

'Eddie and Chloe, please keep quiet!' Mrs Chalmers paused with her piece of chalk in the air. She stopped writing and fixed the Mean Machines with a look. 'We expect silence when other people are reading. You two can behave better than that.'

Yeah, *right*, thought Cy. He stood up. It was his turn. Mrs Chalmers smiled at him and Cy relaxed a little. He always felt better when he knew no-one was going to rush him. He flipped open his notepad, took a deep breath, and then looked down, ready to read out the great ideas he had scribbled down last night. 'Ah . . . ga . . . ahh,' he stuttered.

Matt raised one eyebrow. 'Sorry?'

'Ahh . . . umm . . . nothing,' said Cy.

'Nothing?' said Matt. 'Really?'

Cy nodded blinking back tears. His notebook was empty. Someone had torn out the pages where he had written down all his wonderful story ideas.

'Surely not, Cy,' said Mrs Chalmers. 'You're usually so good at making up stories.' She strode across the room and took Cy's notebook from his fingers. 'Oh,' she said, as she saw that the pages were blank. 'Oh well, never mind.' She gave Cy a consoling pat on the back. 'Never mind,' she said again. 'If you do think of anything, then let us know.'

'Next!' called Matt.

Chloe bounced out of her seat as Cy shuffled away. Her look of triumph as she went by told Cy all he needed to know.

'What's wrong?' Vicky asked him as he slumped down in a chair near the back of a hall.

Cy opened his mouth to tell her, and it stayed open as he heard Chloe read out from her notebook in a loud voice.

'I think that there should be a Saxon princess . . . and maybe . . . maybe . . . she could be running away from some Vikings . . .'

'That's my story!' gasped Cy. 'She's nicked my story!' He looked at Vicky in horror. 'I should have realized someone had been in my holdall. I pushed it right under the bed last night and this evening it was sticking out from under the edge. They must have taken the pages out of my notebook and copied them into their own. How could anyone be so rotten?'

'They are horrible and mean, those two,' agreed Vicky. 'Couldn't you remember any bits of it to tell Matt just now?'

Cy shook his head slowly. He wasn't good at thinking clearly in a stressful situation. He gazed at the stage with a stunned expression on his face.

Matt was talking to Chloe, who was acting all bright and happy.

'I suppose you've got your eye on the part of the princess?' he joked.

'I think I could manage to act as a Saxon princess. Well, I'd do my best,' Chloe said, in a syrupy pretend-nice voice. She began to mince around the stage waving an imaginary fan.

Matt laughed. 'You'll need some direction, Chloe, I don't know if Saxon princesses carried fans.'

At the end of the session Mrs Chalmers came over and sat beside Cy and Vicky. 'Cheer up, Cy,' she said. 'You can't be the best at stories every time. We're going to see the big Viking exhibition in the Jorvik Centre tomorrow. Perhaps you'll see something there that will give you some story ideas.'

CHAPTER·8·

'Pay attention, everybody,' Mrs Chalmers called out.

It was the next day, and Cy and his classmates were waiting in line outside the Jorvik Centre for Mr Gillespie who had gone to buy the entrance tickets.

'There's a huge queue for the Time car-ride,' said Mrs Chalmers, 'but we can go in and look at the exhibits just now, and they'll let us know when it's our turn to go on. We will visit the shop *afterwards*,' she added firmly, as she led them downstairs.

Cy wandered around with his friends looking at the ancient pieces of pottery and housewares. There was a mock-up of an archaeological research lab, and some display boards with audio tracks. Cy picked up the earphones beside one showing the Historical Timeline and stuck them on his head.

'Well, you certainly took your Time in getting here,' said an irritated voice in his ear.

'Dream Master?' said Cy. He pulled the headset half off and looked around. There was no-one beside him.

'Where are you?' asked Cy.

'In the headset, obviously.'

Cy hesitated. He put the earphones back over his ears. 'I can't see you,' he said.

'Do you usually "see" voices?'

'You can't be just "a voice",' protested Cy.

'Why not?' said the Dream Master's voice in Cy's ear. 'Why is it that nowadays humans have to categorize everything? You've become too analytical. There's no *respect* any more. That's what's missing. A bit of respect for the unknown. In the old days people feared.'

'Feared what?' asked Cy.

'Well, practically everything,' said the Dream

Master. 'Life was simpler. People believed in the Legends. They knew where they were with Myth and Mythology. Now with this modern generation, it's scientific evidence and second laws of thermodynamics. Your basic dream just won't do. They're wanting phasers and quasars, pulsars and sonic saypatience.'

Cy thought for a minute. 'You mean Playstations,' he said.

'I know what I mean,' snapped the Dream Master. 'In Olden Days they just believed. It meant that I could do anything, go anywhere. I could turn up in broad daylight, throw a thunderbolt, and everybody did as they were told. If you did that now you'd get arrested. All my dreams are full of stroppy kids questioning everything.'

'It's probably because of science,' said Cy helpfully.

'Science. Shmience. Only last week I had an eight-year-old – an eight-year-old! – telling me what I could and could not do. "This is not logical," he said. "Who needs logic?" I said. "I'll terminate your programme," he said. He threatened me. Me! One of the most powerful Dream Masters ever. It was me who kept the Sleeping Beauty going for all those years.'

'I thought the Sleeping Beauty was a fairy-tale,' said Cy.

'See what I mean?' said the Dream Master bitterly. 'Now I've got a bolshy boy who thinks that one of my masterpieces is a *fairy-tale*. A disobedient dunderhead who is told to wait in one place. And does he do this? No! When I return, *he's* done a runner.'

'That wasn't my fault,' said Cy. 'The Viking dream kind of drifted away, and left me back in the twenty-first century.'

'Well, it's fortunate, by my brilliant powers of deduction, I worked out that your teachers would bring you here . . . eventually.'

Cy glanced around. 'How long have you been waiting?' he asked.

'How long?' said the Dream Master. 'Long? About three furlongs give or take a kilogram.'

'I meant how long in *time*,' said Cy.

'Oh, I see what you mean,' the Dream Master laughed. 'You don't measure Time like that.'

'How do *you* measure time?' asked Cy.

'You can't.'

'I don't understand.'

'Time is completely fluid. Think about it. How long does something horrible last? For ever.

How long does something good? No time at all. How long does your birthday last? Eh? How long does the day *before* your birthday last? You're not going to tell me you actually believe that both those days last the same number of minutes?'

'Well, yes,' said Cy. 'It's just that because one is more exciting than the other they *seem* different.'

'Why?'

'Because nice things seem to be a shorter length. Bad times seem longer. Good times seem shorter,' said Cy.

'Why?'

'Oh, I don't know why!' said Cy in exasperation.

'Gotcha!' The Dream Master crowed with pleasure. 'Answer this one then. How do you measure the time spent with your Grampa?'

Cy couldn't answer. 'I don't,' he said eventually.

'There you are then!' said the dwarf triumphantly.

'For goodness sakes!' shouted Cy.

His Dream Master was becoming as bad as grown-ups for yabbering on. Worse even than his older sister Lauren and her two friends, who could go on longer than any international peace talks.

'Tell me how to end this Story,' said Cy

impatiently. 'We have to stop it before something serious happens.'

'Something serious is already happening,' said the Dream Master. 'This story is moving out of its own time and space. It is beginning to overlap, cause disturbances elsewhere which could alter the timeline . . .' The dwarf's voice tailed off, and Cy heard again a faint note of fear. 'You have to finish it off,' said the dwarf after a moment, '. . . before it finishes you off.'

'What do you mean, "before it finishes me off"?' said Cy.

'I told you,' said the dwarf. 'Because . . . by now it's a nightmare. And although with ordinary nightmares you always wake up . . . eventually, with this one you might not. If you go back into the dream, rather than the dream being in your head, then there's no guarantee that you can come out again.'

'If I go back,' Cy said slowly, 'how do I end the Story?'

There was silence. Then Cy heard the sound of static through the headphones. 'I don't know exactly.' The Dream Master's voice came from far away. 'You're going to have to work out how to do it by yourself. But you must go back into the dream properly the way you began, through the piece of dreamsilk. Take the piece of dreamsilk, and try to reconnect with the Viking dream at the place you left it. Then—'

The crackling increased. It buzzed in Cy's ears and drowned out the Dream Master's words. Cy took off the headset and shook it. He stopped as he noticed one of the staff giving him a strange look.

'Having trouble, son?' The attendant came over and twiddled the knob. He took the headset and put it to his own ear. 'There you go.' He handed it back to Cy. 'It's working fine now.'

Cy put it to his ear. He could hear a recorded tape of historical facts. 'I'm finished, thanks,' he said. He replaced the earphones on their stand and turned away.

CHAPTER·9·

Mr Gillespie was waving the tickets and calling on everybody to follow him to the entrance to the Time Ride. Cy trailed along at the end of the line of his classmates, his mind churning over and over.

He knew that his unfinished Viking dream was seeping through into this reality. He didn't need the Dream Master to tell him that strange things were happening, and . . . Cy glanced uneasily over his shoulder . . . they seemed to be happening in his vicinity. It was almost as if the dream was

following him, seeking him out, trying to reattach itself to him in some way.

'Now you will travel back in time . . .'

Cy started. Who had said that? Ahead of him stood a figure in Viking dress.

'Pay attention, everyone,' said Mr Gillespie. 'The Centre guide wants to say a few words.'

'You will be taken back to when the city of York was known as Jorvik. Underneath the streets of our modern city, archaeologists discovered houses, workshops, and other remains of the town as it was in those Viking times.' The guide dressed as a Viking began to usher them on two by two. 'Sights, sounds, and even smells have all been recreated to give an authentic vision of York in the Viking age.'

Suddenly Mrs Chalmers tutted. 'We seem to have lost Eddie and Chloe. I'm going back to look in the shop. Cy, can you go in that last car by yourself, please?'

As Cy got in his time-car, the attendant reached up and tapped the TV security screen which showed the view down the tunnel. 'On the blink today,' she said. 'It must be these thunderstorms we've been having. It keeps blipping on and off.'

Cy's time-car moved off, then turned and reversed so that he was travelling backwards, back through time. The centuries slipped away quickly until the timber houses, the little shops, and the wattle and daub huts appeared. Cy leaned forward to get a better view as a reconstructed Viking town appeared.

The streets were lined with craft workshops of different kinds: leatherwork, shoe-making, and jewellery. Here was a shopkeeper haggling with a customer, there was a man trading goods, several rings adorning his fingers and a whorled pendant hanging around his neck. Joints of meat were hanging up outside the houses, and pigs burrowed their snouts in the food scraps flung into their pen at the back of the houses.

A swineherd, thought Cy. That's what I was, a swineherd . . .

From the cesspits and rubbish dumps the strong stink wafted into Cy's nostrils. Outside a fisherman's hut a boy and two men gutted fish, talking and laughing as they worked. They were telling stories. Cy caught drifts of their conversation as his time-car travelled on.

Now there was a family scene, with a woman tending her child as she sat by the open hearth in the middle of the hut floor. The coals glowed and the fire flickered, as she stirred a pot.

Cy's car moved on. The historical part was almost finished. Up ahead he could see the excavations display. The car began to turn the corner on the track.

And then it stopped with a jerk. It must have broken down, Cy thought, an electricity failure. He waited. There would probably be an announcement or someone would come to show him the way out. He peered into the gloom. The car ahead had moved on and was now out of sight. And the car behind . . . Cy twisted around . . . He couldn't see any car following his, and all the lights had gone out.

Perhaps he should get out and walk to the exit sign. He half got to his feet. Just as he did so, the car shuddered and moved forwards. Cy clung to the guard rail as it jerked back along the track.

In the town the thatches were burning, the livestock had scattered, and thick smoke plumed up into the sky. People were running and screaming, but they were trapped in the narrow lanes and alleyways with no way to escape.

Cy turned his head to see better. These special effects were magnificent. How were they doing it? It must be a large screen of some kind. He reached out, but there was nothing there to grasp.

And at that moment there came to him a sense of danger. Suddenly Cy knew that what he was seeing was real. Or had been real, and perhaps still was. Somewhere in time and space, this had happened . . . was . . . is happening.

He could only watch then as the raiders rampaged through the city. Right beside him a man was felled to the ground. Cy heard him moan as his jewelled pendant was ripped from around his throat. Further along the street a young child was caught and captured, tossed over the Viking's shoulder to be taken as a slave. Cy could do nothing, yet still hear and see everything that was happening. He was in it, yet not part of it. The fired thatches gave off dense clouds of grey smoke, screams echoed in his ears. The smell of fear was in his nostrils. He could sense the panic of the stricken town, taste the terror of the animals trapped in the burning building. In the distance two figures were fleeing: one smaller, younger . . . a girl, supporting an old man, both of them trying desperately to outrun their pursuers. And, just as Cy realized who they were, he saw the old man stumble and fall . . .

'Hilde!' Cy reached out, but his hand and arm passed through the scene before him as if it had no substance. This was just like a nightmare – it *was* a nightmare.

Cy slumped back in his seat. There was a bump and his car ground to a halt. A member of staff helped him out. She waved her hand in front of Cy's face and grinned at him.

'I can see you really enjoyed that,' she said. 'Your eyes are glazed over.'

Cy walked in a daze past the displays through to the shop area. He had to go back. He knew that now. After scenes like that there was no way that he could abandon this story. Later tonight, after the theatre workshop, would be a good time to unwrap the piece of dreamsilk and try. What he didn't know was whether he had to do it on his own, or whether his Dream Master would be there to help him sort out this Story.

CHAPTER ·10·

'A story,' said Matt, 'a good story, has certain elements to it. And through stories we can learn about life.'

It was after dinner that evening, and members of the theatre group were working on the Viking saga with Cy and his classmates. Matt was sitting on the stage discussing with them how they could use their ideas and construct a story.

'The way a story is structured can teach you about logic, science, and philosophy. I'll try to explain what I mean,' he said. 'For example if this

was a story about a cloudy day ... which soon turns to rain. The character in your story might put up an umbrella, put on a pair of welly boots, and then go out and stamp in some puddles. That one is very simple and used in a lot of picture books. It shows how things happen ... rain is wet and makes puddles.'

While Matt was speaking Mrs Chalmers had quickly drawn cartoons of rain clouds, puddles, an umbrella, and wellingtons in a line along the top of the board.

'Another thing to watch out for,' said Matt, 'is proper sequencing of events.' He pointed to the top of the blackboard. '*First* we have the rain, *then* the brolly and the wellies, *then* the puddle-jumping – not the other way round.' He grinned at them. 'Don't laugh. I know it sounds babyish and simple, but getting events in the correct order is a basic requirement. A lot of people forget this when they write or tell stories. The story should move forward, and it should fit together as it moves ... Any questions so far?'

Cy put his hand up. 'Do you mean that a story can't just be allowed to happen?'

Matt thought for a moment. 'I think that if it was "just allowed to happen" then it might never get finished,' he said. 'When I'm writing a story I know that I need some kind of plan, otherwise I usually get stuck.' He pointed to the bottom part of the blackboard where he had written out notes from the previous night's workshop. 'It's always helpful to write things out. These are all your ideas. Now we'll try to find a storyline from them.' He picked up the chalk and began to talk through the notes.

As Matt wrote on the board Cy was thinking hard. This was the same thing that the Dream Master had been nagging him about. His Viking dream needed to move forward. At the moment it seemed to be stuck. Every time Cy caught a glimpse of it he saw the same events – the burning buildings, the fire – as though it was caught in a never-ending loop.

'Of course we must not lose spontaneity, flair, innovation,' Matt's voice broke into his thoughts. 'A story can create itself as it goes along, and this happens when the most important factor comes into use . . .' He looked around the room. 'Any guesses as to what it might be?'

'Imagination,' said Cy. 'Imagination is everything.'

Mrs Chalmers beamed at him. 'Well said, Cy.'

'Oh, it wasn't me that said it,' said Cy. 'It was Einstein, actually.'

'And always they must entertain ... thrill, excite, even scare those who hear them,' Matt went on. 'However, if we do find it too terrifying we can always bear in mind that it's not real.'

'Maybe not for you,' Cy said under his breath. The storyline for the Viking saga which Matt was drawing and scripting on the blackboard right now was fiction. But in a different TimeSpace ... Hilde and her grandfather were in desperate danger. Cy looked down at his notepad but he didn't see the words he had written there today. He was remembering the old man falling to the ground as he hurried to escape.

'Cy!'

Cy jumped. Mrs Chalmers had called his name.

'Do you have anything to read to us from your notebook tonight?'

Cy flipped open his pad. He had jotted down a lot of stuff throughout the day, and what's more he had made absolutely sure that he had kept his notepad safely in his rucksack at all times.

'I thought there could be a battle,' he said. 'Maybe the one at Stainmore when King Eadred fights . . . sorry, fought Erik Bloodaxe. And Harald,

72

the Viking's eldest son, could be trying to marry a Saxon princess so that he would have a right to the English throne. Perhaps the story could feature a Viking raid with the townspeople trying to fight them off. Plenty of action, anyway—' Cy's voice grew more and more excited and enthusiastic as he told his story, adding bits as they came into his head.

Matt was scribbling furiously as Cy spoke. 'That would fit in with Chloe's princess who was being pursued by Vikings. We should have more characters, people who will bring the story to life. I'll assign parts to each of you based on the readings you gave last night. You can learn your parts tonight and we'll have a rehearsal late tomorrow afternoon.'

'It's beginning to take shape,' said Mrs Chalmers. She spoke to Matt in a low voice. 'I told you Cy had a talent for this type of thing.'

Matt nodded. 'Yes, this is going to work very well. The primary school children will love it. And if we're going to have a battle scene, I think I know where I can get more props to help us out. In York every year we stage events for the Viking festival of Jolablot, when the Vikings celebrated the end of winter and the arrival of spring. I've helped stage mock fights for this, so I'll be able to borrow weapons, costumes and get volunteer "extras" for our battle scenes. If the weather holds we'll put it on outside tomorrow night.' He turned to speak to Cy. 'Cy, I'd like you to be the narrator of the Saga.'

'Me?' Cy could hardly believe it. 'Me?'

Matt smiled. 'Yes, you. You'd introduce the characters and tell the tale. I think you've got a real empathy with storytelling.'

'I don't know . . .' Cy hesitated. 'I'm not good at reading out in front of people.'

'But that's the point,' said Matt. 'You don't. The storytellers didn't *read* the stories. They told them aloud. And they had a gift for doing it. They had to be inventive and imaginative, as you are. The Nordic ones were known by a special name. A Viking storyteller was called—'

'A skald,' Cy interrupted without thinking. He gave Matt a strange look, and then said, 'Yes . . . I will be the skald.'

CHAPTER ·11·

'Well, look who's here! If it isn't teacher's little Cy-bear-boy!'

Cy's stomach flipped and went wobbly as he heard Chloe's voice raised high above the clatter in the school hostel tuck shop. He had just turned away from the counter after being served and found himself face to face with Chloe.

She leaned forward and flicked his paper bag of sweets. 'Buying batteries to keep you sucking up, Cy-bear-pet?'

'Excuse me,' he said in his best assertive tone of voice, 'I don't want to speak to you.'

'Of course you don't,' Eddie spoke from directly behind Cy. 'You're far too clever to talk to the likes of us.'

Cy swivelled around. Eddie and a couple of his cronies had surrounded him at the back. Cy felt the fluttery panic beginning to spread inside him.

'After all, you say the same things as Einstein, don't you?' Eddie began to mimic Cy's earlier conversation with Mrs Chalmers. "Imagination is everything, Mrs Chalmers." "Well said, little Cy!" "Oh, I didn't say it. It was Einstein, actually."' Eddie laughed sarcastically, and spoke to Chloe across Cy's head. 'We should call him "Einstein Actually".'

Chloe shrieked with laughter. 'That's brilliant, Eddie.' She raised her voice. 'Hey, listen to this, everybody. From now on Cy's new name is "Einstein Actually". That should give us a few laughs,' she went on, 'seeing as how he's a complete duffer at most things.'

Cy's heart contracted and then began to race. He felt his face go red. He shouldn't stand and take this. All he had to do was take a deep breath and speak up. But it was so difficult for him to do that.

Was that why they picked on him, singled him out from time to time for their special treatment?

When he had asked Grampa about this, Grampa had talked to him quite seriously. 'There's always bullies. In the last War they called them Nazis, and we tried to get rid of them, but they're still around. It's part of what's known as the "human condition" but, God knows, there's nothing human about it. There are some folk who pick on those who are different, although often they don't even need a reason. It makes them feel good. These people usually don't have much to say about other things. They can't talk about sport, or films, or books or ideas. It's as if there's nothing much inside them but hate, and it all comes spilling out now and then.'

Cy didn't trust himself to speak, so he tried to push past the Mean Machines. They stood firm and started to jostle him.

'Leave it out,' said a firm voice.

Cy turned. Vicky and Basra were now standing beside him. It was Vicky who had spoken up.

'You lot are pathetic,' she said. 'You're so jealous 'cos Cy's better at the Viking saga than you are.'

'You're as bad as he is,' Chloe snapped back at

77

Vicky. 'Miss suck-up Sally. "Yes, sir. No, sir. Three bags full, sir."'

'Sticky-Licky-Vicky,' added Eddie nastily.

'You two are so ... so ... *juvenile*,' said Vicky loftily. She lifted her head high and turned away. But Cy could see that her face was blotchy pink and she had her jaw clenched.

' "Sticks and Stones",' said Basra bravely. And he and Cy hurried through the tuck shop door after Vicky.

Except that it wasn't always true, thought Cy. Not all of it anyway. Sticks and stones *could* break your bones. That bit was true. It was the end of the rhyme that he didn't agree with. 'Names will never hurt me.'

Because they did. Words were like raw energy: charged with power, able to shock or soothe; harm, hurt, or comfort. Their effect lasted longer than a blow. In cruel hands, a dangerous weapon.

'They need sorting, those two,' said Vicky as they walked along the corridor.

Cy and Basra nodded agreement. They all looked at each other.

'It's like that story we got in Primary Year 5,' said Cy. 'Who's going to volunteer to put the bell around the cat's neck?'

'Yeah,' said Basra. 'Which one of you two is going to sort them out?'

'You mean, which one of you two?' said Vicky.

The three friends started to laugh together.

It was much later that night before Cy felt it was safe enough to creep quietly downstairs to find a place where he could use his piece of dreamsilk to go back into his Viking dream. Everyone, including himself, had spent most of the evening muttering away at their lines and acting out their parts, and now they were asleep. But not Cy; the horrifying scenes in the Jorvik Centre this afternoon had let him know that something had to be done. He just was not sure what exactly.

Carrying his sweatshirt with the piece of dreamsilk still wrapped inside, Cy slid into the empty dining room. Just beside the door the Viking costumes and props were heaped in wicker hampers. Perhaps looking through this stuff would help him get back to his Viking dream. Cy went over and lifted the lid of the first hamper. It contained armour and weapons. He put down his sweatshirt and examined one or two of the items. A large polystyrene sword with an intricate handle design, some long pointed spears, a round shield, a battle-axe, a cardboard helmet . . .

Cy picked the helmet up and turned it carefully in his hands and, as he did so, his eyes caught sight of the blackboard on the stage. Cy gasped and stepped back a pace. Writing had been added since the theatre workshop session. Scrawled across Matt's storyline notes were the words . . . DESTRUCTION! . . . FIRE! . . . DEATH!

Cy's fingers lost their grip on the helmet and it fell from his hands back down into the hamper. The hollow eyeslits gazed at him, the depth of their nothingness drawing him in, making his head swim. As if in a trance Cy reached out to his sweatshirt which held the little fragment of dreamsilk wrapped inside. He placed it on the hamper in front of him.

Slowly Cy began to unwrap it.

CHAPTER ·12·

As soon as his fingers made contact with the tiny fragment of torn dreamsilk, Cy knew something was terribly wrong. For a start it was not hanging limp like any ordinary piece of material would. It was moving. Fluttering in agitation, twisting and turning, thrumming with a strange vibration. And, as he attempted to take a firm grasp of it, a blistering white heat scorched along his fingers. Cy yelped with pain, and tried to snatch his hand away.

But he couldn't. There was a short scuffle as

Cy tried to resist, and then he was dragged in.

And now Time was accelerating away from him, then spinning. Next it was lapping around him. It was movement which did not stop, with no beginning and no end. Changing and turning, sucking him in. And then Cy crashlanded in a rubbish-strewn alleyway in tenth-century York.

'About Time too, you Fat-Headed Fumble-Bumble!' Cy's Dream Master stood over him, arms akimbo.

'Where are we?' asked Cy.

The Dream Master's eyes opened wide in shock. 'Why are you asking *me* where we are? This is *your* Dream, *your* Story. You should know the answer to that question.' He pulled Cy to his feet and peered into his face. 'You *have* given this some thought, haven't you? You did work out a rough story outline, surely? I mean, you didn't just grab the dreamsilk and let it drag you back into the dream any old how?' He stood back as Cy didn't answer. Then he began to stamp his foot in fury. 'Of all the, the . . . Sixty-Seven Stumbling Stupidities. Cy . . . Cy . . . you, you . . . Sieve-head!' he ranted. He dragged his fingers through his hair and bit his beard.

'I couldn't help it!' said Cy. 'It just grabbed me

and pulled me in! Anyway,' he added, 'isn't that what a good story is supposed to do?'

'Of course it is,' said the dwarf. 'Except that in this Story, you're letting your imagination run wild. It needs some discipline!'

'I thought you said that a story had a life of its own,' protested Cy.

The dwarf glared at Cy. 'This is the very last dream I do with you ... you ... rebellious ... raconteur. *You* are telling the story, so you need to have some kind of grip, a sort of overview.' He looked at Cy for a long moment. 'You haven't thought about it at all, have you?'

'I have thought about practically nothing else,' said Cy truthfully. 'I was worried about the raid, the fires, and there is one Viking in particular—' He broke off as he heard the sound of running feet.

Cy dived down beside a rain barrel at the corner of a house. Someone had stopped at the end of their alleyway. The figure cast a long shadow on the ground. It had the shape of a tall warrior wearing a helmet. Cy shrank back and squeezed himself as far behind the barrel as possible. The man advanced slowly down the lane looking cautiously from side to side, eyes glaring out from the eye sockets of his helmet. He had almost reached Cy's hiding place when from behind him came shouts and the clash of metal, sword on sword. He swung around and ran back the way he had come.

Cy relaxed slightly, trembling with relief. He hadn't got a clear look at the man's face, but he was almost sure that it was the Viking who had thrown the axe at his head and kept appearing in his waking dream. Had he caused his figure to appear just now by speaking about him? Cy didn't know.

'You're not doing this properly!' shrieked the Dream Master. 'Stories need structure. This is completely out of control! Stop it! Now!'

'I can't,' Cy whispered.

The Dream Master glared at him. 'Well, do *something*! You can't have characters running about all over the place.'

Cy peered out from his hiding place. To him, running seemed a very good idea at the moment. Any second now someone else would come this way and catch sight of him wedged in behind this rain barrel, and he didn't reckon his chances if they did. He recalled that Hilde had said something about a path to the river, a way to safety. At the other end of the lane, away from the noise of battle, he thought he saw the glint of light on water. He grabbed the Dream Master's arm. 'I think the river is that way, and Hilde said there was a path.'

'Hilde?' snapped the dwarf, snatching his arm back. 'Suddenly we have a Hilde. Who is Hilde?'

'Ummm,' said Cy. 'Someone I met in the first dream. A girl. A Saxon princess.'

'You *must* start thinking about this story cohesively,' said the Dream Master. 'Is her character really necessary?' he demanded. 'Does she fulfil a useful purpose?'

'Yes,' said Cy, remembering the axe which had just missed his head because Hilde had elbowed him out of the way. He glanced from side to side. The alleyway was empty. 'I'm going to make a run for it,' he told the dwarf. And before the Dream Master could reply Cy got to his feet and raced off down the lane.

'I'm too old for this,' gasped the little man as he puffed after Cy. 'Slow down.'

Cy didn't check his speed. Without stopping he belted round the corner at the end of the lane, and ran right into someone.

'Owwfff!' yelped Cy and fell over backwards. When he caught his breath he looked up.

A very annoyed Saxon princess, her blue eyes bright with anger, stood in front of him barring his path to the river.

CHAPTER ·13·

'**C**oward!' she spat at him.

'No,' said Cy. 'I'm not ... I wasn't ... I mean, I amn't.'

'You ran away to save yourself,' Hilde sneered at him.

'It wasn't like that,' Cy stuttered.

'You left me alone to help an old man to safety.'

'I left you ...' Cy thought desperately. He could feel his street-cred slipping away fast here. Then he remembered the Viking warrior, and some vague idea about chivalry and damsels in distress came

into his head. 'I left you ... to ... to stay behind and ... er, joust for your honour.'

'Ignorant Idiot!' the Dream Master's voice hissed in Cy's ear. 'That's straight out of King Arthur. You're with the *Vikings*, remember?'

Hilde looked at Cy as though he had gone right off his rocker. 'What nonsense are you talking now?'

'They broke through the front door,' said Cy thinking quickly. 'There was a Viking warrior, a huge man. He came towards me swinging his sword. It was a terrifying sight, but I stood my ground. I managed to hold them up for a few precious seconds to give you time to get away.'

'Oh,' Hilde hesitated then, unsure. 'Oh ... well, then ... I thank you.'

Cy uncrossed his fingers. Technically it was true. He *had* delayed their pursuers a bit. She didn't need to know that what in fact had really held the Vikings up was the falling roof beam clonking Harald on the head.

'Forgive my rudeness,' she said reluctantly.

'Oh, all right.' Cy tried not to sound too smug.

Hilde turned away and knelt down beside her grandfather who was sitting in the grass by the river.

'There was a terrific fight,' Cy went on, anxious not to lose his advantage. He had to show this bossy girl that he was as good as she was.

'Uhuh,' said Hilde. She had dipped a cloth in the river and was bathing her grandfather's face.

'Yes,' said Cy. 'Arm-to-arm combat; we struggled for ages. This man was about ten feet tall,' he added.

'I doubt that,' said Hilde.

'No, really,' said Cy, thinking that now, for once, he had the perfect opportunity to use his imagination. 'He towered over me, eyes flashing with hatred. He had the strength of six men, at least.'

Hilde opened her own eyes very wide.

'You have no idea,' said Cy.

'But I do,' said Hilde calmly. 'For I know the man of whom you speak quite well. He wishes to marry me, but my family have refused. This is why he pursues me. His name is Harald, eldest son of Erik.'

'Oh,' said Cy.

'Oh, indeed,' said Hilde. She stood up. 'You should be a skald instead of a swineherd. Your stories are very entertaining.' She pointed at her grandfather. 'You help Grandfather. I will go ahead and make sure the way is safe.'

Cy went over to help the old man to his feet. As he leant down to offer him his arm he looked into his face. Eyes deep with wisdom looked back at Cy. The expression was so like his own Grampa's that Cy caught his breath.

The old man reached out a frail hand and Cy gave him his arm to lean on. Cy made a rude face at Hilde's back as they set out after her, through the long grass.

Hilde's grandfather chuckled as he saw Cy's expression. 'You *are* a good storyteller, boy. Don't be ashamed of it, it is a great art.'

Storyteller! Cy's heart jumped as he remembered the reason he was here. He was supposed to be finishing this story off properly. He had to dream up a satisfactory ending, and he'd better do it right away. Cy quickened his pace to catch up with Hilde.

'Listen.' He caught at her sleeve. 'Stop a moment, I have to think what we are going to do.'

Hilde shook herself free from Cy's grasp. 'I know exactly what we are going to do. We will find somewhere safe to hide until nightfall, and then make our way southwards to the camp of King Eadred and his army. But, for the moment,' she glanced anxiously around her, 'we must avoid being captured by Harald, Erik's son.'

'Too late for that, I fear,' called a voice behind them.

Cy and Hilde turned together.

On the path behind them stood a Viking warrior. It was a figure Cy recognized at once. Tall and helmeted, in one hand he held his war sword, in the other, his battle-axe.

'You are surrounded by my men,' said Harald. 'Give up at once. The old one cannot run and the boy cannot fight.'

'Perhaps *he* cannot,' Hilde's breath tore from her in a long ragged sound, 'but *I* certainly can!' And she flung herself forwards at Harald like a frenzied wild cat.

CHAPTER ·14·

At least one good thing will come of this, thought Cy, as Harald's men grabbed the snarling Hilde and dragged her to one side. It gets her off marrying him. There's no way that he's going to go for her after that.

Harald wiped the blood from the scratches on his face. He smiled grimly at Hilde. Then he stepped forward and struck Hilde's grandfather a blow which sent him to the ground.

At once Hilde stopped struggling. 'Infamous bully,' she shouted.

'I will have you, willing or not,' said Harald.

'It is not me that you want,' cried Hilde. 'It is kingship that you seek, and you think that you will find it by marrying me.'

Harald laughed in such a way that caused Cy to shiver. 'You are right,' he said. 'I seek your hand neither for your looks nor temperament. Your uncle, King Eadred, is marching north with his army to drive us Norsemen from this land. My father Erik, famed for his mighty axe, and I, Harald, his first-born and heir, will do battle with him at Stainmore. There we will kill him and wipe out his army. Then, royal child, I will marry you and in time I can claim rights to all this kingdom.'

'Never!' shrieked Hilde. 'I will never marry you!'

Harald looked at her coldly. He moved nearer Hilde's grandfather and raised his sword slowly. 'One should respect the aged,' he said, 'and I know that he is no threat to me, as being by your mother's side he bears no royal blood, yet . . .' He placed the point of his sword at the old man's throat.

'Don't!' Hilde cried out.

Harald's eyes narrowed and he surveyed her carefully.

'Please,' the word came from between Hilde's teeth.

Harald lowered his sword. 'Very well,' he said. 'Now let us be gone from here. We must make haste to reach my father.' He glanced at Cy. 'Deal with the boy,' he ordered one of his men.

Cy staggered back. What did 'deal with' mean exactly? He looked at Hilde. Her mouth had dropped open.

'We need the boy with us,' she said quickly. 'He tends my grandfather.'

'You can see to the old man yourself,' said Harald curtly.

'I . . . I . . . I'm not important,' said Cy feebly. 'I'm only a swineherd.'

'Yes,' said Harald. 'I guessed as much. I saw at once that you had no skills in fighting. Therefore, you are of no use to us.' He nodded at the man closest to Cy. 'Get rid of him.'

The man nearest Cy drew a long knife from his belt.

Cy felt his insides becoming like hot liquid. He looked around wildly. He was on his own and there was nowhere to run. Why did the Dream Master always disappear when he needed him most?

'He can tell stories,' said a voice suddenly. It was Hilde's grandfather who had spoken up. 'Imagination and dreams come alive through his words. I have heard him. They are good stories . . .'

Harald went close to Cy and gazed into his face. 'You are a skald?' he asked.

Cy forced himself to look back. He stared into eyes half-crazed with war and power, and tried desperately not to blink.

'Yeum,' he managed a strangled gasp. It was true. Matt had said that he had a gift for story-telling. Cy nodded his head. 'I am a skald.'

'Tell me one,' said Harald. He gave an evil grin. 'Tell me a story to save your life.'

Every story Cy had ever known slid right to the bottom of his brain. 'I . . . I . . .' His voice tailed off. Don't panic, don't panic, don't panic, he told himself. It was no good. He never operated well under pressure, and this certainly equalled any class exam he'd ever taken.

There was silence. Time hung like a drop of water from a leaky tap.

And as Cy watched, he knew the exact micro-second that Harald's patience ran out. He saw it in his face, in his eyes. But, just as Harald's attention began to slip, the moment before he started to look away, Hilde had a coughing fit.

'I'm sorry,' she spluttered. 'So sorry . . . forgive me, Cy. Please begin again. What did you say?'

Cy stared at her stupidly.

Hilde tried again. 'I thought I heard you speak. Didn't you say . . . "There was once a famous Viking . . . ?"' She rolled her eyes at Harald and then back to Cy.

'Ah yes,' Hilde's grandfather broke in at this point. 'I too recall that story. It was about a proud warrior.' He looked at Cy, then stared hard at Harald, and then looked back to Cy.

They're trying to help me! thought Cy. He felt a sudden surge of relief. He should tell a story . . . about a Viking warrior. 'Once upon a time,' he said quickly. 'Once upon a time . . . er . . . the Viking, Erik, famed for his mighty axe, came across the bleak North Sea in many longships. Longships with high sails and prows of painted dragon heads . . . They came, they saw, they conquered . . .' Cy improvised frantically as he tried to remember what Mrs Chalmers had read out to them on the bus as they were travelling to York. 'And this Erik fathered many sons, each of them mighty warriors . . .' Cy noticed that Hilde was nodding her head vigorously towards Harald. Of course!

Harald! 'Particularly the eldest,' Cy went on. 'He was the mightiest, first-born, number one, the main man,' Cy risked a quick glance at Harald. His lips were curved in a half smile. 'He was Erik's heir, and would inherit all his lands and wealth. Erik, whose famous axe ran red with blood, known in song and story as Erik Bloodaxe . . .'

'Erik Bloodaxe!' Harald interrupted. He turned to his men. 'That is good. I like that. From now on my father will be known as Erik Bloodaxe, and I am the main man.' He thumped Cy on the shoulder. 'You are indeed a skald,' he said. 'And we will need a good storyteller to give the account of our victory at Stainmore. You will use the best words you know to tell about my deeds of bravery and skill in battle?'

Cy nodded weakly.

'Good,' said Harald. 'Then I will spare your life – for now.'

CHAPTER ·15·

Cy kept a tight hold of the piece of dreamsilk
as he was hauled along the river path with
Hilde and her grandfather.

'Why do you keep looking back?' Hilde asked
him. 'Do you have friends who might follow and
rescue us?'

'I thought I had a friend,' said Cy bitterly. Why
was it that when things got really bad the Dream
Master was nowhere to be seen? At scary
moments he always managed to duck under his
dreamcloak and vanish completely. 'But he

seems to have mysteriously disappeared.'

'Then we must try ourselves to escape.'

'How?' asked Cy.

There were armed men to the front and rear. Hilde and himself might have been able to dodge away and escape among the grass and bushes, but Hilde's grandfather would never keep up. And Cy knew that neither of them would leave him behind.

'They will stop to eat and rest for part of the night,' said Hilde. 'Then we must take our chance.'

'Thank you for helping me out earlier,' said Cy. 'Telling them I was a storyteller was a good idea.'

'A debt honoured,' said Hilde, 'for your help to us. And it was not all untruth,' she added. 'At times your speech is fanciful and . . .' she glanced at him and smiled, '. . . entertaining.'

Hilde's grandfather nudged Cy. 'She likes you,' he whispered.

Hilde's prediction was right. At the next hamlet Harald called a halt. The people had run away at their approach, and the men foraged in the huts for food and firewood.

Harald took Hilde roughly by the arm. 'You, girl, and your grandfather can stay and eat with me by the fire.' He laughed. 'Give the pig boy some pig food and put him in one of the huts for now.'

It was almost completely dark in the hut and it took Cy a moment or two to realize that he was not alone. A small figure sat cross-legged on the floor.

'Oh, so now you decide to reappear,' Cy said sarcastically.

'Don't criticize what you don't understand,' said the Dream Master.

Cy picked up a piece of the stale bread which had been thrown at him.

'Yecch,' said the dwarf. 'How can you eat that?'

'Believe me, it tastes better than the stuff they were getting in Eadred's army.'

'Ah yes,' said the dwarf. 'Eadred and his army . . . They are not many miles distant from here. I will show you the way there and you can finish this dream with them at the battle of Stainmore.'

'Stainmore?' said Cy. 'You want me to go to Stainmore and be with King Eadred and his army?'

'Yes, yes,' said the dwarf testily. 'That's where you began, isn't it? Marching with Eadred's army?'

'I can't leave Hilde and her grandfather,' said Cy. 'She needs my help for them both to escape.'

The dwarf raised his eyebrows. 'Is this the same

Hilde who scratched Harald's face and almost gouged his eyes out?'

'He is going to force her to be his wife so that he can claim the throne of England.'

'There are more polite ways of turning down an offer of marriage,' said the dwarf.

'He threatened to kill her grandfather!' cried Cy.

The dwarf leaned close to Cy. 'That is none of your business,' he hissed in a low voice. 'You started this dream off with Eadred's army. Switching viewpoints in a story is a bad idea. So now you must go and rejoin the army, and end the dream there.' He walked to the door. 'Come, I will show you the way.'

'No,' said Cy. 'I can't just walk away from this.'

'Then run,' suggested the dwarf. He opened the door a crack and peered out. 'You may have to.'

Cy shook his head. 'No.'

The Dream Master turned to face Cy, then he frowned and reached forward. 'This dream is getting thin.' He touched the hut door again. His hand almost passed through it. 'Your focus is beginning to slip. Has something stressful happened to you recently?'

'Stressful!' said Cy. 'I've been captured by a band of Vikings whose leader is a lunatic and who has threatened to kill me at a moment's notice. I would call that stressful – yes!'

'All of that,' said the Dream Master, 'is entirely your own fault. But that kind of excitement shouldn't affect your dreamweaving. If anything it should make it more vivid . . . No, has anything traumatic happened in your ordinary, dull, humdrum, everyday, rather boring existence, which by the way, I try to liven up now and then by giving you a really interesting dream? Think twenty-first century Real Time. Did you have a bad experience lately?'

'Well, sort of,' said Cy. 'I had a run in with the Mean Machines.'

'Fifteen Fiddlesticks!' said the dwarf. 'Them again! I should have known that there was a reason you were having so many problems with this dream. Your concentration has been faulty from the start, and now the whole thing is beginning to drift away again.'

Cy looked around him. Through the walls of the hut he could very faintly see the walls of the hostel. They were moving, gently swaying . . . No, it was his dream that was moving. He tried to concentrate. The air shimmered slightly. Cy pulled the piece of dreamsilk from his sleeve. It was washed-out grey, and the dream itself was now floating gently, tugging like a tethered balloon. His dream had moved in space. There was now a distance between it and his reality.

'Some of your dreamtime has to be used to sort out daytime events,' said the Dream Master. 'Part of your mind must still be taken up by whatever happened with those two bullies.'

'But that happened during the day,' said Cy. 'It's over. It doesn't affect me now.'

'Of course it does! It all meshes together. Do you understand nothing?' The dwarf peered at Cy. 'Oh, I keep forgetting, you're stuck in that dreadful twenty-first century where most people are still locked into thinking that everything exists in linear dimensions. It's not like that. Don't you see? It *all* relates. Einstein managed to grasp the concept. But it isn't just time that's relative. *Everything* is relative.'

'Relatives,' repeated Cy. He thought of Grampa and his sister, Lauren. They were relatives. The dwarf's image was fading. He could hardly hear his voice.

'Your dream energy is running low, like sand in a glass. You're going to have to leave this dream and come back again. Get out, Cy. Get out. Now!'

'Relatives,' said Cy again. They said you could choose your friends, but not your relations. But that wasn't completely true. Friends chose you, or didn't in some cases. He realized that he was now getting really mixed up. 'OK,' he said to the dwarf. He took the piece of dreamsilk and looked at it. It was pearly translucent. Cy staggered to his feet. He had better go while he still could. If the dream moved further, then he could be trapped here for ever. Gripping the dreamsilk firmly in his fingers Cy stumbled to the door and pulled it open.

CHAPTER ·16·

Cy walked out of the hostel dining hall and bumped into Mr Gillespie.

'Cy!' exclaimed his teacher. 'What are you doing down here at this time of night?'

Cy rubbed his face in a daze.

Mr Gillespie looked at him closely. 'I think you're sleepwalking. Let me get you a drink and then I'll take you back to the dormitory.' He took the scrap of dreamsilk from Cy's fingers. 'You won't need that,' he said, and he dropped it into the open wicker hamper by the door.

When Cy woke the next morning he only had the vaguest recollection of his Viking dream. And he found that he couldn't think about it much anyway because there was something else nagging at his mind. All through breakfast, as they collected their packed lunch bags and then waited for the bus to take them on their day trip, there was something he should know, or had to remember, but what? He knew that it was important, but that didn't help at all. In fact, it often made things harder to recall. The more urgently he needed to do something the greater was the chance of it slipping down one of the cracks in his brain. It was a familiar feeling for him. Often when he was sent on errands, or to collect something, he completely forgot what he was sent for. Quite frequently the original message got mysteriously replaced with another completely different one. So that once, when he was sent to the shops for a loaf, he came back with a packet of soap powder. He'd never forgotten the expression on his mum's face when he'd handed it to her.

'Wakey, wakey, Cy!' Mr Gillespie waved his closed fist in front of Cy's face. 'How many fingers am I holding up?'

'Oh, ha, ha, sir,' said Cy.

'Ha, ha, yourself on to the bus,' said Mr Gillespie. He turned to Mrs Chalmers. 'This lot are half asleep today.'

'They've been up half the night, learning and re-learning their lines for the play tonight,' said Ms Tyler.

'They never take anything we do at school as seriously,' said Mr Gillespie.

'It's because Matt is bringing his professional actors along tonight to mingle in their crowd scenes,' laughed Mrs Chalmers. 'They think that they'll be talent-spotted and end up at the Cannes Film Festival or winning an Oscar.'

'Ah, that explains a lot,' said Ms Tyler. 'The amount of make-up passed around the girls' dormitory last night would have done the cast of *Gone With the Wind* three times over.'

'Poor Cy must be so nervous about his part as the skald. I found him sleepwalking last night,' said Mr Gillespie.

Cy's ears opened up at the mention of his name. Sleepwalking? Him? Last night? 'Oh, no!' he whispered, as the events of the previous night came rushing back in a flood, and with it a tide of rising panic. One memory stood out clearer than the rest. He turned and began pushing his way back down the bus.

'I have to get off,' he said desperately. 'There's something I need to collect.'

'Sorry, Cy,' said Mr Gillespie. 'We're booked in at the Railway Museum, and we're late already.' He closed the door and signalled the driver to pull away. 'Sit down. Now!' he ordered as Cy dithered in the passageway of the bus.

Cy slumped down in his seat. 'Don't panic, don't panic, don't panic,' he muttered under his breath. He almost wished that he hadn't remembered what he had. But the terrible fact was in his head and would now not go away. Instead of having his piece of dreamsilk tucked away safely inside his sweatshirt and crammed at the bottom of his holdall, it was now lying in Matt's wicker stage props hamper.

The visit to the Railway Museum went in slow motion for Cy. The huge engines, the massive works of engineering, the interactive displays hardly made any impression on him. When they sat to watch the film and video presentations he found that he couldn't concentrate at all. His overriding anxiety was completely centred on the piece of dreamsilk. He was first back on the bus, and grabbed a seat right at the front. It was only as Mrs Chalmers led the rest of the class on to the bus that Cy realized that meant he would be sitting right next to her.

'Well, Cy-bear-pet's a real teacher-toady today,' whispered Chloe as she came on the bus.

'Shut up,' said Cy. 'Princess Chloe Clappermouth!'

'Cyrus Peters!' exclaimed Mrs Chalmers. 'It does surprise me to hear you talk like that.'

'She started it,' said Cy, as Chloe went smirking up the bus.

'Well, that does NOT surprise me,' said Mrs Chalmers quietly.

Cy looked at his teacher in astonishment. She winked back as she settled herself beside him. 'I've got my eye on her,' she said as she picked up the P.A. mike.

When the bus stopped outside the hostel Cy jumped to his feet to be first off, and then realized that the driver had opened the middle doors at the same time. As he got caught in the surge towards the hostel Chloe elbowed her way close beside him.

'You watch out,' she said. 'Nobody calls me names and gets away with it.'

'Yeah.' Eddie was now on his other side. 'You need putting down.' He nodded across at Chloe.

'I don't have time to talk to you,' said Cy, and he pushed past them and raced towards the dining hall. He shoved the door open and ran inside. Matt was standing by the hamper. The lid was flung back and he was just about to reach down and pick up the Viking helmet. He glanced up in surprise as Cy appeared at his side.

'Here, let me help you,' Cy's voice was taut with stress. He put his hand into the hamper and lifted the helmet. Curled inside it was the dark fluttering piece of dreamsilk. With a quick movement Cy took it and thrust it into his packed lunch bag.

'Rehearsals in half an hour,' Matt called after Cy as he hurried away.

Outside the door Cy stopped and took in a deep breath. Now he had to avoid the Mean Machines, but first he should put the dreamsilk in his pocket. He began to open up his lunch bag.

'Cy!'

Cy jumped as he heard his name called. Mrs Chalmers was standing in front of him. She had a serious look on her face.

'Can you come into the hostel office please?'

Chloe and Eddie were standing beside the desk.

They had on their most innocent expressions.

'Cy,' said Mrs Chalmers. 'Chloe has lost a silver pendant which she bought at the Jorvik Centre although,' Mrs Chalmers paused and gave Chloe a firm look, 'you were told not to shop at that time. At any rate, Chloe says she dropped it as she left the bus, and Eddie thinks he saw you pick it up and put it in your packed lunch bag.'

Cy gasped. The Mean Machines must have cooked this up between them on the bus. That was why they had jostled him so closely on the way inside. One of them had slipped the pendant into his lunch bag. Cy glanced down into his paper carrier. Nestling among the orange peel and half eaten crisps he could see the gleam of silver. 'Oh, no!' he whispered, and he felt his face go red.

'That's exactly what I said.' Mrs Chalmers had taken Cy's strangled whisper for a denial. She reached over and plucked the paper carrier from Cy's fingers. 'Let's just settle this right away,' she said briskly, and she upended the bag.

Cy closed his eyes. And so he missed the looks of triumph on Eddie and Chloe's faces changing to ones of puzzlement as Mrs Chalmers searched among Cy's lunch leavings and failed to find the pendant.

'Just an old piece of black cloth and some rubbish. I think you two owe Cy an apology.'

Cy opened his eyes slowly as his teacher spoke. What had happened? He was sure he had seen the pendant in his bag. It couldn't have just disappeared. Could it? And then Cy noticed the piece of dreamsilk lying on the desk, and realized that it could have – not disappeared exactly, but slipped from one TimeSpace to another. When Mrs Chalmers emptied his bag the pendant must have fallen into, and through, the dreamsilk. The piece of black silk lay unnoticed on the desk, and to Cy it seemed to quiver, vibrating, charged with energy.

'Cy ran away into the dining room as soon as he came inside the hostel,' said Chloe quickly. 'He could have hidden it there.'

Mrs Chalmers clicked her tongue in annoyance. 'Cy,' she began, 'did you—?'

'No,' Cy spoke up at once. 'I swear I didn't. I'd left something there last night and I went to pick it up. You can check with Matt if you like. He was in the room with me.'

'But the pendant was definitely in his bag,' Eddie burst out. 'We know because—' He stopped as Chloe kicked his leg.

'Because . . . why?' Mrs Chalmers asked in an icy voice.

'Because I saw him put it in,' said Chloe.

Mrs Chalmers' eyes narrowed. 'But that's not what you told me at first, Chloe. You said that you had lost your pendant, and it was Eddie who saw Cy pick it up.'

'I . . . I . . . yes that's right,' said Chloe.

'We're just mixed up about how it happened,' added Eddie.

'Getting "mixed up" about something as serious as this is *extremely* unwise,' said Mrs Chalmers in a dangerous voice. 'Perhaps I should telephone Cy's parents. They might want to sue you for defamation of character. I will think about that and let you know what I decide. In the meantime,' she raised her voice and spoke loudly and distinctly, 'I want to hear no bad reports about either of you for the rest of this trip. If you two look sideways at anyone I will deal with you myself.' She waved her hand and dismissed them. 'Now go.'

'And you can go too, Cy,' she added kindly after Eddie and Chloe had slunk out of the room. 'If those two start any more mischief, come and tell me quietly and I'll sort them out.' She made to gather up the debris on the desk. 'I'll throw this stuff away for you.'

Cy leaped forward and grabbed the piece of dreamsilk. 'Need this,' he garbled. 'Prop for the play, sort of.' And as he left the room he stuffed his little bit of precious dreamsilk deep into his trouser pocket.

CHAPTER ·17·

And it was still in Cy's pocket later in the evening when Matt fastened the long flowing storyteller's cloak around him, and pinned it at his neck with an ancient whorled Viking brooch.

Matt stood back and adjusted the folds until he was happy. 'OK?' he asked Cy.

Cy nodded. Even though they'd spent two hours rehearsing, his throat was closing over with nerves and he didn't trust himself to speak. 'Don't worry about it.' Matt punched him on the arm.

'You'll be great.' He pointed to the make-up table in the boys' dressing room. 'Do you want any make-up on?'

Cy shook his head.

'Thank goodness for that,' grinned Matt, ''cos I don't think there's any left. Now go for a walk outside and mingle with the audience. The kids from the primary school along the road are sitting on groundsheets in the big field down by the river. Try to wind them up a bit about the story. Got your note card?'

Cy nodded again. Matt had printed all their parts out on the computer so that they could read them if they got stuck. Cy stuck his card in the pocket in the folds of his cloak and wandered outside. Matt's actor friends in Saxon and Viking costumes were already walking about among the crowds. They had brought all their equipment in a horse-drawn cart. Matt had told Mrs Chalmers that they would be useful to make up the numbers in the battle scenes. Some of them helped run the Battle Drill for the Children's event at the York City Jolablot Festival, where they taught youngsters Viking combat skills. He'd said it could be quite spectacular how they handled their special weapons, and that they'd probably show off a bit with their battle techniques.

Cy moved around the field. Soft shadowing evening was creeping up on day. The sun caught the glint of the coloured ribbons and metal foils and threw the light back at the sky. The rest of his class were gathered at one end behind a rigged-up theatre curtain. They were having noisy sword fights with each other. Cy was so restless that he could not even watch, far less join in. He went back indoors and sat in the boys' dressing room.

Matt stuck his head round the door. 'Better now? You go on in five minutes, but Mrs Chalmers is doing the cues, so she'll give you a call.'

Cy shook his head. 'I don't know. Suppose I forget what I'm supposed to say?'

Matt looked at him and grinned. He waved his hand in the general direction of the field outside. 'Shall I tell *them* to ad lib then? Let the characters do just what they want? I had to take a firm line with Chloe to make her give up her fan! Just think what she might do with no-one restraining her!'

Cy shuddered.

'Exactly,' said Matt. 'Anything *you* say has to be better than that.'

Cy could imagine the performance his class-mates would put on if they were allowed to write their own parts. The Dream Master was right. For unconstructed stories – think 'chaos' and 'shambles'.

Matt smiled at Cy. 'If you get stuck, just do what every other storyteller I know does. Make it up as you go along. As long as you remember the outline then a bit of flair and imagination never go wrong.' He gave Cy a quick wave and was gone.

Cy caught sight of Vicky as she went past the door. She smiled at him. 'Break a leg.'

'You too,' said Cy.

'Doesn't it just make you puke that Chloe is the princess?' Vicky made a gesture of sticking two fingers down her throat.

Cy laughed and made gagging noises.

'Why don't you just retell the story so that something majorly awful happens to her? After all,' Vicky called back over her shoulder, 'you *are* the skald.'

'Yes,' said Cy aloud. He turned and looked into the make-up mirror. 'Yes,' he said again. 'I *am*, amn't I?'

'Please do NOT get carried away with yourself here,' said a peevish voice.

Cy blinked. The Dream Master had appeared, sitting on top of one of the hampers in the corner of the room.

'This is a piffling little production in a farmer's field, for heaven's sake! I mean, *dahling*, London West End, it *isn't*!'

'What are you talking about?' asked Cy.

'Come on,' said the dwarf. 'I can see it in your eyes. You're stage-struck! The lure of the lights. The smell of the greasepaint . . . the roar of the lion.'

'*Crowd*, actually,' said Cy.

'Whatever.'

'I'm not anyway,' protested Cy. 'I was just thinking about being the skald though . . . and about my Viking dream. The story has got to go the way the skald says . . .'

'The story goes like this,' said the Dream Master nastily. 'Cy goes back to his Viking dream.' He pressed his face closer to Cy's own. 'And then Cy returns to march with the army of the English King Eadred who—'

'No!' cried Cy.

'Yes! Yes!' The Dream Master stamped his foot. 'Don't you understand? If you decide to change your Viking dream then I cannot help you.'

'I am going back to *exactly* where I was previously,' declared Cy. 'I cannot abandon Hilde and her grandfather.'

'Then you are on your own,' said the dwarf. He stood up and very abruptly he drew his dream-cloak around him.

Cy sat for a moment thinking things out. It seemed obvious now. He had to be in command of the dream, not the other way around. *He* would have to direct the dreamsilk, not let it lead him. And . . . he glanced quickly at his watch. He didn't have much time. He had to do it now.

Slowly from his pocket Cy took the piece of dreamsilk. It quivered softly in his fingers. Then very gingerly, and with great care, Cy laid it out on the palm of his hand.

CHAPTER ·18·

The little fragment of dreamcloak vibrated gently. Cy let it ripple through his fingers. He could see himself in the long mirror which hung on the back of the dressing-room door. Beyond his own image was the make-up table with its own mirror above it. The double image reflected the table on which lay the cardboard Viking helmet ... which turned slowly on its axis.

'Ah!' Cy gasped, and his heart leaped like a stranded fish.

How could it turn like that? A cardboard helmet

couldn't move by itself. Cy twisted his own head around. The cardboard helmet was still, unmoving, on the make-up table. Cy turned back to the mirror. In the mirror beyond, the helmet head was swivelling slowly, turning to face him . . . Cy's throat closed with fear. He knew what was about to happen. In a few seconds he would see the nosepiece, the eye sockets, and then that murderous look would blaze forth at him. His head spun. The helmet seemed to get bigger, enlarging so much that it filled the mirror, moving upwards, looking down on him from a great height.

Cy squinted up at the figure which towered above him.

'Waken up, swineherd skald.' Harald kicked Cy not very gently in his ribs. 'We have almost finished eating, and now we want a story. You will tell us a tale to see us through this night.' He stretched down, hauled Cy to his feet and shoved him through the hut door out into the night.

The Viking warriors were grouped around a great fire, and moved aside to let Cy sit among them.

Cy chose a position near Hilde and her grandfather, and looked around him anxiously. The Dream Master had said that he would not come to help, but . . .

'You didn't see a small dwarf by any chance?' he asked Hilde.

'Dwarves are maggots,' said a warrior sitting close by, 'born of the flesh of Ymir, the Frost Giant.' He glared at Cy suspiciously. 'I met a dwarf once in a dream I had, where fearsome dragons with many people swallowed in their great bellies, roared and blew out smoke. We do not want to know of dwarves.'

The man next to him hit him across the back. 'No, Ivar, you misunderstand the boy, he is beginning his story.' He leaned across and cuffed Cy in a friendly manner. 'Tell us the tale of the small dwarf.'

'Eh?' Cy's head was ringing. If that was a friendly push, then heaven help him if they started getting rough. He looked more closely at Ivar. He was the Viking whom the Dream Master had saved from being run over by the City Tour Bus in York! No wonder he was suspicious of dwarves.

'The dwarf,' prompted the other man. 'Tell us the story of the little man.'

'What little man?' Cy looked around him in bewilderment. 'Where is he?'

The Viking roared with laughter. '*You* tell us,' he said. 'Begin at the beginning.' He took a long drink and wiped his hand across his mouth. 'What is his name?'

'Actually,' said Cy, as a thought occurred to him, 'I don't know if he has a name.'

The Vikings around the fire looked at each other uneasily. 'A man with no name? How can that be?'

'Swineherd,' said Hilde in a low voice, 'if your life depends on your storytelling, then prepare yourself to meet your gods – soon.'

Cy looked at her blankly.

'Each thing, on the earth and under it, must be named,' said Hilde. 'Else it cannot exist. They think that what you say is an ill omen. Do not speak unwisely here on the night before a battle, not if you wish to see the morning.'

The Vikings were whispering to themselves. One or two had laid their hands upon their swords or axes.

Don't panic, don't panic, don't panic, Cy told himself.

Harald turned his mad eyes towards him. 'What is this story you have to tell us about a little man who keeps his name a secret?'

'Oh no!' thought Cy. Now he would have to tell them another story first, before the real one which he had planned. What story could he tell them quickly about a little man who kept his name a secret?

'If you *dare* call me Rumplestiltskin, I'll sue,' said a familiar voice in his ear.

A great light switched itself on inside Cy's head. '*That* story. Yes, indeed, that is a very good story,' he gabbled. 'It's called Rumplestiltskin. There was once a miller who had a daughter, and he told everybody that she could spin straw into gold . . .'

'I do not like that story,' said Hilde, when Cy had finished. 'The daughter should have kept the gold for herself.'

'No, no,' said Harald, 'the king must have all the gold. You are a great skald, boy. I am glad that I spared your life.' He laughed out loud. 'Tomorrow we shall all have gold!' He raised his axe in the air and began to sing.

Cy and Hilde whispered together as the flames leapt up in the darkness, and the Vikings' voices rose in a great battle-song.

'I think I might know a way to get us out of here,' said Cy quietly.

'We cannot escape,' said Hilde. 'Harald has put a tether rope around Grandfather and tied him to his own wrist.' She glared defiantly at Cy. 'I will not go without him.'

Cy smiled at her. 'Nor will I,' he said.

CHAPTER ·19·

Cy knew that the most important thing was the Time. He needed to get it just right . . .

'I know what you are planning . . .' said an irritated voice.

Cy turned his head. The Dream Master stood directly behind him.

'. . . and I'm telling you now, it will never work. Firstly, what makes you think you have the skill to manipulate that piece of dreamsilk like that? And don't forget, you're due on stage in the school hostel field in about three minutes Your Time.'

Cy clenched his hands tightly. What was it his Grampa always told him? 'Never mind if other people don't have confidence in you, try to have confidence in yourself.' Cy gazed resolutely back at the little man. 'And that is exactly where I intend to be.' He looked around nervously. 'Although I may have company with me . . . temporarily.'

'You *do* know the meaning of the word "temporarily", I trust?' sneered the dwarf.

'If you're not going to help, then go away,' said Cy rudely.

'No way,' said the dwarf, 'to use a twenty-first centuryism. A morbid curiosity compels me to stay. Definite disasters do delight—'

'Shut up!' said Cy. 'You're wasting precious time.'

The dwarf withdrew a few paces away in a huff.

'What are you whispering about?' whispered Hilde.

'I'm getting ready,' said Cy. He turned his head to look directly into her bright blue eyes. 'Do you trust me?' he asked her.

She looked straight back at him. 'No, not really,' she replied. She heaved a sigh. 'But . . . my choices are somewhat limited, so . . .'

An edge of daylight was beginning to show

along the horizon. Around the fire the Vikings were stirring themselves to make ready for the coming battle.

Cy spoke low and urgently to Hilde, 'Go with me on this, and *please* do exactly as I tell you.'

Then Cy stood up and raised his arms high above his head. 'I have a story,' he said, 'a tale to tell of heroic deeds, of a glorious battle fought and won by mighty men.'

Harald and Ivar raised their heads and looked at Cy. Harald nodded approval. 'Yes, this is good,' he said. 'We will have a glorious battle.'

Cy glanced upwards at his own wrist, where he could see the face of his digital watch. Quite soon now Basra would be reading Cy's cue line. Cy grasped the dreamsilk. 'In a faraway land,' he stated determinedly, 'called Schoolhostel, there lived Hilde, a blue-eyed princess, and her grandfather . . .' Cy paused. Was that enough? Did he only have to mention them once to get them back with him into the Viking Saga story in the twenty-first century?

'Don't forget yourself, Sieve-head Cy,' murmured a not unkind voice.

'. . . and Cy, the swineherd skald . . .' Cy added quickly. He looked again at his watch. The numbers hadn't clicked round. 'What's happening to my watch?' he muttered out of the side of his mouth to the Dream Master.

'This may come as a surprise to you, but they don't have digital watches in tenth-century Northumbria,' said the dwarf.

'Blast it!' shouted Cy. He pulled his watch from his wrist and threw it down on the ground.

Both Harald and Ivar grabbed for it at the same time, and as they did so Cy realized that his piece of dreamsilk had caught in the strap.

'No!' he shrieked.

Too late.

There was an almighty crack, a rush of splintering white light, and then they were falling, tumbling through TimeSpace, to land with a thud on the playing-field of the school hostel.

Harald was first on his feet. 'Where is this place?' he snarled. 'How have you brought us here?'

'You're in my story,' said Cy nervously. He reached out quickly and snatched back the watch and his piece of dreamsilk. 'You have to do what I say,' he added quickly.

'Oh there you are, Cy!' Mrs Chalmers came hurrying over. She grabbed him by the arm.

'You're on. Now!' She gave him a little push as he hesitated.

Hilde's grandfather raised his hand and addressed Mrs Chalmers. 'Good lady,' he said. 'What place is this?'

'The school hostel,' said Mrs Chalmers. 'And if you've come to see the Viking play then please hurry up and find a seat.'

Ivar put his hands over his eyes and began to moan. Harald let out a roar.

'Quiet please,' ordered Mrs Chalmers briskly. 'Sit down there on the grass at the side and listen to the Viking Saga.'

'A Viking Saga,' Harald repeated the words carefully. He took off his helmet and looked round in confusion. Then he passed his hands across his face. 'Am I dreaming?'

'Yes,' said Hilde. She sat down, and the rest followed her lead.

As Cy began his Saga, Hilde took her grandfather's hand and began to edge away from Harald. Harald gave her an evil grin and held up his wrist. He still had the tether rope attached.

At the front of the audience Cy announced the Saxon princess. Chloe swept out from behind the curtain and began to overact dreadfully.

'Oh my,' she simpered. 'Someone save me from these awful Vikings.'

'Here is a noble Saxon princess . . .' said Cy.

'I *don't* think so,' said Hilde loudly.

Chloe glared at her. 'Yes I am,' she said. 'It's *my* part. *I* am the Saxon princess.'

Harald stood up at once. 'You *are*?' he said.

'Yes,' said Chloe firmly. 'Definitely. I get captured by the Vikings.'

Harald's eyes narrowed. He took his knife from his belt and cut the rope which bound Hilde's grandfather to him. Then he advanced on Chloe. 'I do not mind exchanging one for the other. You seem more biddable and can be no more unpleasant than the squalling cat I captured earlier.'

'Don't be too sure about that,' Cy muttered under his breath.

As Harald approached Chloe, she stopped speaking suddenly and pointed at him. 'You're wearing my pendant,' she said. 'Give it back to me.'

Harald looked down at the pendant which was hanging round his neck. 'I found it,' he said. Then he gave a wicked grin. 'But certainly you may have it if you wish. Come here and I will give it to you.'

Chloe marched across the stage.

'Oh, no!' said Cy.

Harald grabbed Chloe and hoisted her high up in the air. Then he swung her almost upside down over his shoulder. Her scream was long and terrified. He ran to where the horse and cart was standing and flung her inside. Then he leaped up, grabbed the reins and made off across the field, nearly running down Ivar who had tried to follow him.

Ivar shook his fist. 'Road rage!' he yelled and chased after him.

'Omigosh,' said Cy. 'Omigollygosh.'

'Keep on storytelling, my good swineherd skald,' said a voice in his ear, 'and I'll attempt to rescue Chloe Clappermouth.'

The audience clapped and cheered. 'Amazing acting,' said Mrs Chalmers. 'That Viking looked so real.'

Matt nodded. 'Their costumes are absolutely authentic,' he agreed. 'But they do tend to ham it up a bit.' He looked at Cy. 'Can you cope?'

'I'm short of a princess for this story,' said Cy.

'No you're not,' said Hilde, and she stood up and marched out in front of the audience. 'Now,' she demanded, 'which Viking thinks he is going to take me prisoner?'

'I do,' said Eddie.

'I wouldn't if I were you,' said Cy.

'But you're not me,' said Eddie. 'And I'm capturing the princess.'

And he stepped forward, bravely if rather stupidly, Cy thought.

Hilde seized a polystyrene battle-axe and delivered a resounding thump to the side of Eddie's head. He staggered and fell down. The audience roared.

'Anybody else?' asked Hilde.

There was some shuffling among the Vikings as Cy's classmates all tried at once to move as far away from Hilde as possible.

'Control yourself!' Cy hissed at Hilde. 'You're *supposed* to get captured.'

'Says who?'

'*I* do,' said Cy. 'And I'm the skald. So either you do it my way, or I'll call Harald back.'

Hilde hesitated, and then crossed to where Basra was standing. 'Capture me,' she ordered him.

'Emm . . .' Basra hesitated. He looked up at Hilde and then across at Cy. 'Should I?' he asked.

Cy threw away the note card which Matt had printed out for him and began to ad lib furiously . . .

CHAPTER ·20·

Later, much much later, Cy, Hilde and her grandfather trudged wearily by the side of a great forest. Cy glanced sideways. Although he had never once complained, it was obvious that the old man was very tired. It had been really very late last night before everything had been packed up and put away. Hilde and her grandfather had waited patiently hidden in the trees down by the edge of the river until Cy had come with his piece of dreamsilk to take them to safety. Now they were back in the tenth century – but where?

Cy looked all around. The path went on for miles with no sign of any shelter. He had been trying for what seemed like ages to dream up York so that they could return to their own town. But it just wasn't happening. What was he supposed to do with her and her grandfather? He couldn't take them back again into the twenty-first century. Yet he couldn't just walk off and leave them to fend for themselves.

'We should rest,' he said.

Hilde pointed with her hand. 'There,' she said, 'there we will rest. At the crossroads.'

'Crossroads?' Cy blinked. He couldn't see a crossroads. In fact he could hardly see at all. Harald's helmet was way too big for him, but he did like wearing it. Cy took the helmet off and looked again. There *was* a crossroads . . . had it been there a moment ago? He looked at Hilde. She gave him a brief smile.

'I too can make good stories.'

'Oh,' said Cy.

'Oh, indeed, swineherd skald.'

At the crossroads they could see in the distance a stretch of water and the straggle of huts that showed the start of a township.

Hilde stopped. 'This is where our lives part, swineherd,' she said.

Cy stared at her. 'King Eadred has defeated Erik Bloodaxe at Stainmore. The Vikings will leave now, so you are no longer in danger. I thought that you would return to your relatives in York ... er ... Jorvik?'

'I am not going back to live as before,' said Hilde. 'If I return to my uncle's household then I will be bartered as a bride to whoever pays him the best price. And I will not be in thrall to any man.'

'What else can you do?' asked Cy.

'I will leave England,' said Hilde. 'Many years ago Grandfather journeyed to a far land on the rim of the western sea, and he has always wanted to return. Some call it Vinland. Strange plants and fruit, and all manner of things such as we have never seen, grow there. The weather is kinder, the seas are full of fish, and travellers tell stories of wondrous sights, huge lakes and falling water.' She looked at Cy shrewdly. 'You also are a traveller, I think. Though what lands you travel in I do not know.'

'Neither do I a lot of the time,' said Cy.

She smiled, and then she pointed to a rough track which led away through the trees and into the forest. 'That way leads down to the river, and to a boatman that my grandfather knows. Together we will find some means to travel back to Vinland, and there we will live, with no-one to tell us what to do.'

Cy shook his head. 'I can't let you do that. It's far too dangerous.'

Hilde put her hands on her hips. 'I do not recall asking your permission.'

Hilde's grandfather chuckled. 'Better not to argue, boy. I never do.'

Cy hesitated and then he held out his hand. 'Good luck.'

After a moment Hilde took his hand awkwardly in her own. 'Good luck for you, swineherd skald.' She turned away quickly and, taking her grandfather's arm, she began to walk along the track which led to the forest. When she reached the first trees, she looked around, waved and was gone.

'I hope she'll be all right,' said Cy as the two figures blurred and disappeared in the darkness of the wood. 'They are very brave to decide to go and live in a new land.'

'Don't you know anything?' said the Dream Master. 'Vinland is North America. Just think . . . shopping malls, freeways, drive-in movies, inter-state trucking . . . she'll have a ball.'

'Doesn't all of that come a bit later on?' said Cy.

'At this time North America has hostile tribes and ferocious animals.'

The Dream Master swung his cloak. 'I wouldn't think any of that would bother Hilde too much. Believe me, she's capable of asserting herself anywhere.

'Meanwhile . . .' he peered into his cloak, 'I'd better go and rescue Ivar.'

'Ivar?' said Cy. 'I thought you'd taken him and Harald back to Stainmore?'

'Emm, not exactly,' said the dwarf. 'Harald missed the battle. You'd've thought he would have been grateful, not getting killed, but he was so angry with me that my concentration slipped and I let Ivar slip into another TimeSpace.'

'Where is he?' asked Cy.

The Dream Master peered into his dreamcloak. 'Wandering around the Millennium Dome.' He leaned over and tapped lightly on the top of the Viking helmet. 'Don't forget to bury that in the right place,' he said. Then he swung his cloak and disappeared.

Cy walked on by the river into York, and back along the path he had been dragged along when captured. When he reached the burnt-out shell of Hilde's grandfather's house, he took off Harald's helmet and carefully hid it in the midden pile. There it would be safe. Almost certainly no-one would look there, not for a long, long time.

CHAPTER · 21 ·

'Last chance shopping trip,' Mrs Chalmers announced as they were packed and ready to leave on the Friday morning, 'apart from Eddie and Chloe. You two still need time to recover from your dreadful ordeal. Matt says that sometimes the actors do get a bit carried away.' Mrs Chalmers looked with very little sympathy at Eddie and Chloe. 'Both of you can have a nice rest while everyone else is in the shops, and then sit with the teachers on the bus all the way home.'

Eddie said nothing. He still looked a bit stunned, thought Cy, but then being walloped round the head by Hilde would leave anyone feeling fragile. Chloe opened her mouth and then closed it again. She was exhausted, what with having had to walk ten miles back from outside the town. She had told a story about a little dwarf in a black cloak stopping the runaway carriage and then disappearing with Harald into thin air. Nobody believed her, and hardly anyone would listen to her any more.

'Right,' said Mr Gillespie. 'We'll have one hour in the Coppergate Shopping Centre, and then home!'

Everyone gave a big cheer. Cy noticed that the teachers cheered the loudest.

And now, as he walked along the Coppergate, Cy knew exactly where he was going. The Jorvik Centre was just a few minutes' walk away. He could buy his souvenirs in the shop there. Also . . . there was something in particular that he wanted to see.

The shop and exhibits were not too crowded and he managed to find some free space in front of the glass case which held the helmet hologram.

It revolved slowly in front of him. Cy thought it was stunningly beautiful, and now not threatening at all. The domed crown, the nose-guard, the intricate design. He stepped back to take it all in, and collided with someone standing just behind him. It was one of the Centre guides who was renewing some of the display boards.

RECENT EXCAVATIONS IN CANADA the sign read.

'They've proved that the Vikings were in North America before Columbus,' said the Centre guide. 'These are photographs from recent excavations.'

Cy looked at the display panels. So this was Vinland, land of falling water and tall trees. There was a photograph of a dig with a group of archae-ologists grouped round a Viking tomb. Something about one of the figures seemed familiar. Cy peered closer at a young woman standing holding a Viking battle-axe. He saw her fair hair ... blue eyes. Recognition struck like a hammer blow. 'Hilde!' he cried.

The Centre guide gave Cy a strange look. 'Do you know her?'

'Yes, no, well ... maybe,' said Cy. 'Who is she?'

'She's Ingrid Hilde, one of the foremost Canadian Viking experts. We have a lot of contact with her. She believes her ancestors came from York and settled in Canada centuries ago. That some great-grandfather was related to a Saxon prince.'

'Grandmother,' said Cy, 'definitely grand-mother.'

So maybe all of it was true, Cy thought when he was back on the bus. He looked up at the City walls for a moment as they passed through Monksgate. And maybe you couldn't really define stories. The way they worked was different depending on who told it, and when you heard it. If you heard the same story years later, then you would have the memory of its first telling buried in you. Stories were special, moving like the sea with deep places and quiet shallow waters. Each story was unique, as unique as every human person.

Cy tucked the bit of paper with the Vinland website address on it into his top pocket. The piece of dreamsilk was safely wrapped up in his sweat-shirt down at the bottom of his holdall. Cy took out his notepad and pencil. Mrs Chalmers had said that there would be prizes for stories written about their Viking trip. She had also said that it was a very good idea to begin your story with something happening . . . 'Action before Reaction' she called it. First make things happen, then do the whys and wherefores after. Or, as the Dream Master might say, *let* it happen. The story should be allowed to go its own way.

So, thought Cy . . . he should try to have an event first. Supposing he made it begin with dialogue? Dialogue with something happening . . . something fast. Say someone in danger . . . they could be running away.

Cy smiled to himself. He knew exactly how his story would begin. He gripped his pencil tightly and began to write.

'Move!' shrieked the girl . . .